The Golden Whip

His heart hammered a wild tune as his eyes slid from yellow gold to pale silver, and then to the brilliance of giant diamonds.

"It fair turns a man's head," Martin Chandos whispered.

"A captain's share for you, Martin Chandos!" Redscar shouted. "It was you who gave this to us! Now what do you say to being a buccaneer captain?"

Lizzie's eyes lit with violet fire. "Yes, Martin! Yes!" she cried.

Martin Chandos still stared at the treasure, the sea wind playing in his long brown hair.

A roar rose from the crew, and they crowded round him, dirty and bloody, begrimed with gunpowder and spray. Their laughter was a hot and rousing thing, and the smell of salt air was in his nostrils, and gold and silver and jewels lay at his feet.

He swung on them and spread his hands. "Now, damn you, I'll be your captain, if that's your wish. But at sea, my word is law. Obey me, and I'll make every unwashed man jack of you rich beyond his dreams!"

MADAME BUCCANEER

by
Gardner F. Fox

GOLD MEDAL BOOKS
FAWCETT PUBLICATIONS, Inc., NEW YORK

First Printing, August 1953

MADAME BUCCANEER

Chapter One

THE BLACK GALLEON came down on the wallowing East
Indiaman in a sliding rush that sent half a dozen frigate
birds lifting and dipping over the heavy waves. Her dark
hull was gilded at curving beak and towering sterncastle,
and a tall gold cross glittered over her bowsprit, below
the white sails bulging on the towering masts. A puff of
white smoke appeared at her prow, and an iron shot went
arching over the blue waters to fall into the waves with
a splash.

An instant later, the big man on the poop deck of the
fleeing cargo ship heard the muffled thud of the cannon.
Martin Chandos fastened his hands to the rail and
pulled, as if he could urge the Forthright to a faster pace
by sheer strength. His face was lean under the long brown
hair that hung almost to his shoulders, and his skin was

baked, by long exposure to the sun, to the rich color of Honduras mahogany.

The Forthright owned four demicannon, brass pieces set on wooden mounts and lashed to the rails by hempen ropes. The great black galleon, the Vengador, carried sixty guns, with pairs of sakers at beakhead and stern.

His fist hit the rail capping as Martin Chandos shook bitter laughter into the wind. "There's peace between Spain and England in this year of '65, but she means to take me. We've no more chance to beat her than Tighernmas had before the golden idol of Crom Cruach!"

But the hot Irish blood that beat faster in his veins at thought of a battle brought him to the main deck, stripping off his brown coat of coarse homespun wool and the cotton shirt beneath it. He bared a deep chest, and great wide shoulders under which the muscles moved as if alive.

He took an ax and went to a crate and worked arm by elbow with Peter Horne, his sailing master out of Sussex. They lifted out muskets to the eager hands of the crew that ringed them in.

The sailing master grunted, "You mean to fight them, then?"

Martin Chandos paused to breathe in the air that was tangy with sea salt. "I fought them before, with Penn and Myngs, but then we served under the Protectorate, and I had more than four demicannon to use. Still, if the Shee fairies grant us a bit of luck, we might give an account of ourselves!"

He took his post on the poop, above the whipstaff hutch. His voice carried to the sailors swarming in the rigging. "Hoist your foretacks. You, helmsman, hard aport!"

The Forthright swung clumsily, but she came about to the wind, just as the gunners on the Vengador were putting linstocks to the touch holes. Now the narrow stern of the East Indiaman faced the galleon, and the broadside that lifted the Vengador, intended to smash the cargo ship in one mighty onslaught, went harmlessly into the sea, except for two iron balls that ripped into the stern cabin.

"Lash down those guns!" bellowed Martin Chandos from the rail. "I'll set them myself!"

As the cargo ship luffed about to present her port side to the emptied cannons of the Spaniard, Martin Chandos placed his guns. He set them high, so that he might do the most damage with what he had. Matches flared, and were held to touch holes. The little cannons roared, recoiling on their wheeled mounts.

Their shot tore through the proud white sails of the Spaniard. One ball hit the towering mainmast below her flag, and the cracking sound as the oak mast splintered carried over the waves. Broken, the snapped mainmast came down with its ropes and rigging, tangling the main course in a ruin of parted ropes and ragged sails.

The Vengador veered.

On the East Indiaman, sweating men were dousing barrels with water, and shoving iron shot into cannon chambers. Martin Chandos grinned and bent to his task, aligning each gun with steady hands, head craning forward to study his target.

The Forthright drifted past the great gilded sterncastle of the galleon. Slowly she swung until her port rail faced the Spaniard's rudder. With a grim smile on his lips, Martin Chandos brought the flaming linstock down. The gun erupted.

A wave lifted the Vengador and dropped her in a trough of water. But for that, the iron shot that was aimed from the cargo ship would have splintered her big wooden rudder into a thousand pieces. But the galleon was dropping down, and the shot went high, to fall with a clatter of smashing glass above the stern post.

The Forthright seemed to groan as the wind caught and drove her slowly by the swinging galleon. Her chance was gone. The black ship came about, and now her larboard guns were spitting flame and smoke, and iron shot and langrel swept the rigging of the smaller ship.

Martin Chandos stood in the rain of canvas and rigging, a big ax in his hand. He said softly, "They'll hammer us to pulp, and then they'll come aboard."

Twice more the Forthright belched their own balls at the galleon, and twice they brought confusion to the Spaniard. As Martin Chandos set and fired each gun, the cargo ketch fought back. But the odds were too much for the slow East Indiaman. The galleon splintered her sides and smashed her masts and made of the sails and rigging a twisted ruin across her bloody decks.

The Vengador's grappling irons gleamed in the sun as they arched through the air to bite into the wood of deck and rail. Spanish muscles dragged the little vessel close, and an orderly wedge of soldiers in breastplates and morions came yelling over the sides.

The fight was short and bitter. Flying splinters of wood and metal had wounded half the crew. Spanish muskets and steel hacked the others down, from the larboard rail to the poop deck.

They took Martin Chandos with his back against the wooden door of the stern cabin, their swords marking his chest and arms with trails of blood, took him with a metal hilt crashing down across his head, with the long barrel of a boarding pistol thudding hard between his eyes. And even then his great body rose up against the pain and the blackness that was flooding it. He came forward two, three steps, and his ax swung once before his blind eyes and a Spaniard screamed as it drove into his throat.

Martin Chandos toppled like a tree before the wind on the hills of Kenmare, and went face down on the bloody planking of his dying ship.

The boarders dipped buckets overside and doused him back to consciousness with stinging salt water.

A lean man came forward, ominous and grim in the silvered corselet and morion that reflected the faces of those who gave away before him. A foot of Mechlin lace was at his wrists, and the rich black velvet of hose trunks and cape gave him the appearance of a nobleman playing at war. But there were a bloody gash on his chin and a powder stain on his sleeve. His eyes were brown and somber as they regarded this man who had cost him more than the last five ships he had put at the, bottom of the *Mar del Norte*. A smile twitched at his thin, wide mouth.

"*Mis felicitaciones, señor!* The compliments of Don Carlos Esquivel Alcantara on your fighting kinship with the god of war."

Martin Chandos shook his head until his long, wet hair flapped at his throat. His blue eyes were hard sapphires in his browned face. Only the fact that two Spanish soldiers stood at each arm kept him from hurling himself at this sneering hidalgo.

"If I'd had the deck of the Centurion underfoot, or that of the Marston Moor, it's not on Mars you'd be calling, you blackhearted spalpeen!"

Don Carlos lifted his brows. "The Centurion? You

fought, then, with Christopher Myngs? Ah? Then we are well met, señor! I fought myself at Coro."

Martin Chandos growled, "There is peace now between Spain and England! A peace you violate here on the high sea."

"Oh, but Captain! There is peace only in the Old World, where court protocol demands such formality. Here, in this wide, wild wonderful world that belongs to Spain, there is no peace. No peace between Spanish gentlemen and foreign bastards!"

Don Carlos Esquivel Alcantara lifted a languid hand, shaking back the foot of white lace that sheathed it, to touch the tiny black mustache on his upper lip. His eyes brooded on the big, bronzed man who faced him so boldly. And then they were lit by a hard, sneering glitter.

"I find you in need of a lesson, Captain. An introduction, shall we say, to the mastery of Castile. Spain has put an iron curtain around the Indies. A curtain of iron shot and iron shell. Those who penetrate it will meet the fate you are to suffer now."

The lace quivered as his hand waved, and men came and put their hands on Martin Chandos and dragged him across the deck to a gun mount, where they threw him down and twisted cording around chest and loins, at knees and arms, so that he hung spread-eagled on the cannon.

The Spanish captain advanced slowly, until he could stare down into the face of the bound man. For a moment he considered him, then said softly, "You are lucky, señor. I might have had you tied to a metal spit and roasted over glowing coals while still alive. Or taken a rat from my hold, and placed him inside an iron pot upended over your hard belly, to gnaw its way through your middle to escape the heat of a fire lighted on the pot's upturned bottom. But that would kill you. My wish is that you live, to carry word back to your piratical England to stay out of Spanish waters!"

He took the long black whip that a soldier handed him. Almost lovingly his palm caressed the long thongs that were whipped around the horn handle. He shook it out and let Martin Chandos see it.

"A cat-o'-nine-tails, Captain. A most ingenious device with which to flay skin from a man's back. As you shall see, as you shall see."

Don Carlos Esquivel Alcantara threw back the lash from him, into the reaching hand of a burly seaman. He smiled softly. "Instruct our captain, Juan. A few times only."

Living fire wrapped itself over his back and around his ribs. His great body lifted and fell against that searing pain. The whip fell again, and again. It stung with the fury of a thousand claws, but Martin Chandos, after that first convulsive heave, showed no response. He heard laughter, and raised his sweating face.

Don Carlos Esquivel Alcantara was standing with head thrown back, wild laughter screaming from his open mouth.

Between his teeth, Martin Chandos rasped, "You find it amusing, you Spanish dog?"

Don Carlos was discovering that his merriment would not let him speak. He waved a hand, and the whip paused; and when he had caught his breath he said, "Most amusing, Captain! Your back shall be marked for all time, for Englishmen to read the fate that befalls them when they come trading in the lands that belong to Aragon and Castile! Now lay on again, Juan!"

That wild laughter soaked into him as the knout laid his skin and his bloody flesh open as it coiled and landed, and gathered itself to bite again. Soon his back was nothing but raw flesh, with blood splattering the gun and the deck below it. Martin Chandos bit down on his lips with clenched teeth. The whip went on, rising and falling steadily.

How long that lashing continued, Martin Chandos never knew. They threw buckets of salt water over his back, drawing an involuntary scream from his cracked lips. The pain sucked strength from his muscles and left him a limp and dying thing across the gun mount.

The Spanish grandee laughed all through the lashing, laughed as a man might at some most seemly jest. Head thrown back, he roared gustily, or, peering through wet eyelashes, chuckled ever and again as the lash coiled down and landed with a sodden *splaaat*. His mirth came to the man hung spread-eagled over the cannon as acid comes to glass, to etch it. The laughter ate into Martin Chandos, and found some corner of his being where it fed, and, feeding, grew to become one with the pain.

While Don Carlos amused himself with the ship's captain, sailors from the great, black Vengador swarmed below the hatches of the Forthright, brought her cargo of tools abovedeck, and swung them overside into bobbing longboats to be rowed to the dark galleon.

The crew members were tied back to back and made to sidle sideways to the rail, where a push sent them pitching down into the blue waters below. There, hooks from the Vengador's longboats caught their ropes, and they were dragged thus through the water toward the black ship until, half drowned, they were yanked aboard and cast into the darkness of the bilge.

The whip fell to the deck planks. At a gesture from the splendidly garbed hidalgo, the swart executioner ran to the rope ladder.

Dipping his hand into his gold snuffbox and thrusting the brown powder into his thin, aristocratic nostrils, Don Carlos Esquivel Alcantara stared down at the bloody back of the man hung over the gun carriage. For an instant a black cloud of passionate hate twisted his arrogant features. He lifted his boot and brought the heel up hard against the unconscious man's cheek.

"Account yourself lucky, you English dog," he whispered. "For what your people did to the Armada, for what they have done to Spanish subjects—Drake at Darien and John Hawkins at San Juan de Ulua—I should have torn out your heart and made your crew eat it!"

He paused, his slim hand clenched tightly about the silvermounted butt of a long boarding pistol, breathing harshly. It would have taken little to spur Don Carlos into action. But the sun was warm, and the little Forthright pitched and dipped to the heaving waves, and blood dripped steadily from the inert hulk over the cannon to the deck. At last Don Carlos sighed and shrugged and turned toward the rail.

In an hour the Vengador was a black dot on the horizon, and the little brown ship drifted on, while salt water seeped slowly into its rents and holes, dragging it downward toward the bottom at a gentle pace.

Martin Chandos moaned against the pain racking his big body. Once his head lifted and his eyes rolled whitely as he arched his wide back. Standing on spread legs, he tugged at the bonds that made him a prisoner of the gun, aware that the ship was settling under him.

He mumbled through cracked lips, "There's no

strength to my arms. That devil's whip took all of it out of me!"

As if his words exhausted him, he fell forward. His head cracked against the brass barrel and he sagged to his knees on the deck planks.

The brown ship drifted on, sinking slowly.

A huge red ball of a sun bloomed in the orange sky. It baked the shell-splintered railing and half-deck boards, and threw a red coating over the wet sides of the big brown hull. Far to port, a faint blue smudge on the horizon betrayed the island of Hispaniola. Out of sight, sixty miles to leeward, lay the great length of Cuba.

The waves pushed, and the wind played, and the wreck of what had been an East Indiaman out of Plymouth drifted on.

Toward dusk the wind shifted and ran northwestward from the Caribbean to the Gulf. It caught the merchantman and hurled it sideways into the trough of the waves until she pitched like a drunkard to the heave of the gray-blue sea. Waves slapped the high forecastle boards and splattered the main deck with pounding water. The spray of the breaking waves showered the man bowed over the cannon, rousing him from his stupor.

Martin Chandos sniffed the lifting wind, his head like that of a hawk scenting prey. A lock of brown hair slapped his neck and exposed his jutting nose and wide spread of mouth and a face that was the color of old bronze. The glaze had faded from his eyes, leaving them cold and hard.

He chafed at the leather thongs, but only succeeded in slashing his wrists until blood covered the thin leather strips. He used his white teeth on them, baring them like an animal between the stubble on his lips. In his pain and helpless frenzy he hurled himself left and right, yanking backward, striving to free himself by brute strength.

It was in one of these convulsive flailings that he discovered a ship bearing down on him out of the dying sun, looming black and gaunt, silhouetted against the red sky like some obscene monster. Her triangular sail was tight with wind, and his seaman's eye judged her for a small bark. His eyes ran up the shrouds to a ragged black flag on her masthead.

Martin Chandos hung in his thongs and watched the

buccaneer ship veer closer, moving across the gap of surging water between them, close-hauled to avoid the clumsy lunges of the sinking Forthright.

The pirate ship swung broadside on, and now the man at the cannon could read the gilt lettering that spelled "Hussy" on her forecastle boards. Men were spilling down rope ladders into a rocking longboat, men that were half naked, with red scarves twisted around their heads, with pistols stuck into wide leather belts and curved cutlasses hanging by chains from their middles. Oars slid out and backs bent. The oar blades dipped into the blue water and lifted to fall again, and the ship's boat skipped across the waves.

Martin Chandos watched a hand and then a face lift up over the splintered wreckage of the deck rail. Then they came running across the ruin of the main deck.

A knife slid between the brass barrel and his wrist, slicing thongs. A voice growled in his ear, "Spanish work! I'd know its mark anywhere!"

He tried to nod his head and mumble agreement, but they did not hear him. They were intent on forming a sling from the shrouds, into which they fitted him, swinging him overside and lowering him carefully to the tender that bumped its beam against the Forthright's timbers.

As he felt a hard, wet thwart against his bleeding back, the world went reeling in a pool of water and sky.

Martin Chandos did not feel the surge of the longboat through the water, or the gentle hands that lifted him upward past the opened gun-port lids to the carved rail of the Hussy. Those hands steadied him, holding him upright on the deck as a woman came from the companionway to pause abruptly and stare at him in astonishment.

Lizzie Hollister was no grimy ship's wench. Her wide mouth was a red fruit set below a small nose and dark violet eyes, and the wealth of black hair that spilled to her shoulders' skin gleamed, as the dying sunlight caught it, with a reddish glint. Earrings that were strung balls of bright brass dangled from her tiny ears, to match the thick strands of painted metal balls that were draped about her soft throat.

She wore a thin white shirt thrust into a pair of tight black breeches girdled with a wide leather belt, into which a brace of long-barreled flintlock pistols had been thrust. Her long legs, bare below the ragged edges of her breeks, were thrust into bright red boots of Cordovan leather.

. Her violet eyes regarded the man who supported Martin Chandos. He was big, with a mat of reddish hair on chest and shoulders. Two gold hoops dangled from his ear lobes. He was totally bald, and a red scar that ran the length of his right cheek from lips to temple was partially hidden in the crimson beard that framed his mouth.

"Hell-fire!" she said huskily. "Is this all she had, Redscar? Just one man?"

The giant at Martin Chandos' elbow grinned. "And even he bean't in very good condition at the moment."

Her bright eyes snapped at his lewd grin. Redscar Hudson liked this pert hoyden, for all that she was reported to be Sans Espoir's woman. There was a fire in her, and she'd listen to reason, even if Raoul Sans Espoir had taken her on some of his freebooting ventures and it pleased him to think she was worthy of being a member of the brotherhood.

Lizzie strutted to the larboard rail and stared at the yawning Forthright. "No profit in her," she muttered. "She'll go down by the head in a few hours."

Redscar grunted. "The Spanisher that wrecked her took her cargo and crew. He enjoyed himself with this one, whipping him near to death."

Lizzie turned and came back, moving slowly around the limp Chandos. "He's a big ox," she admitted. Her violet eyes studied his deep chest and wide shoulders and the length of the muscled arms hanging by his sides.

Redscar bent his head. He whispered, "All he needs is a mite of salve and bandage, Lizzie. He'll be good as new then."

Her face grew sullen and her red mouth seemed to thicken to her thoughts. She shrugged carelessly, but a little fire began to glow under the wide leather belt that bound her black breeks to her rounded hips.

Redscar caught her thought. "I'll take him below for you, Lizzie. It's your chance to play pirate like Harry Morgan himself. They take their women aft. Why not take your men?"

Lizzie Hollister shook her head, but her eyes were feverish. "Damn your eyes, Redscar Hudson, that see so much! Take him below to my cabin, then. But only that

I can doctor him back to health. He might know things we should learn."

Redscar put a knuckle to his brow, head bobbing. "For sure, Lizzie, for sure. Just for a mite of doctorin'."

His laughter followed her to the companionway.

Chapter Two

MARTIN CHANDOS woke to the touch of fingers upon his lacerated back. He lay flat on his front in a cabin bunk, with the creak of an iron ship's lantern directly overhead. By raising his head he could see the wide span of stern windows, divided by carved and gilded timbers, above the wide cushions fitted to a roomy sea chest inbuilt from bulkhead to bulkhead. A table of Honduras mahogany was set with a brass nocturnal and a boxed mariner's compass on either side of a metal lamp. Beyond the slanting windows, the night lay like a black fog across the waters.

The softness of the fingers that doctored his flesh made him lift his head, and he found himself staring upward into a woman's face.

Her lips twisted in a smile. "Never seen a girl before, laddie?"

"Not on—"

Her violet eyes regarded him steadily, under thin brows that had been plucked to an upward slant. Her lips pursed, and the touch of her hands grew harsh.

"Not on a pirate vessel, you were about to say. Be glad you're under the black flag now, and not the red and yellow of Spain."

Her hair was black and lustrous, with reddish glints in its soft length. She went on. "Redscar told me what the Spaniard did to you. Bound for Jamaica with your tools, weren't you? I've anchored off Port Royal with Morgan more than once."

Martin Chandos lay quiet. What use to tell this female corsair of the Spaniard who had wrecked his ship and clapped his crew below decks, and whipped him until his throat went raw from holding back his screams? This hate and thirst for vengeance was his own, and was not to be shared with a buccaneer.

His silence annoyed the woman. She took her hands away and stretched, straightening. Her violet eyes taunted him as they detected the direction of his glance. When his eyes dropped lower, she laughed out loud.

"Been out of England some weeks, haven't you, laddie?"

Martin Chandos flushed, and turned to put his face on his forearm. He heard her kneel, and then her hands were warm on his bare shoulders.

"Never mind Lizzie. I've as sharp a tongue as I have a dagger. I need them both, to control those things out there. Tell Lizzie what happened. You're master of the Forthright, out of Bristol, with a cargo of tools for the Jamaica plantations."

"Out of Plymouth," he corrected, "with every brass farthing my father left me sunk into her hull and hold. And it was a Spaniard did it to me. In time of peace between our countries! Sinking a peaceful cargo ship, firing on a man who intended no harm to him! He might as well have been one of your own kind, flying the black flag."

The woman came off her knees to stand with her brown hands clenched into hard little fists. "As well be one of my own kind, say you?"

"Aye! A damned buccaneer he was, bad cess to him! A tall man with a thin face and red lips, and a laugh I'll remember from here to hell. That lash played a tune on my back such as Hobgob himself might play on the heights over Kenmare. And at every stroke of that cat, he laughed. I said he was a pirate, and pirate he is! Just like yourself, but not so honest."

Lizzie Hollister was rigid. "Buccaneer! Pirate! Fine words from a man who owes his life to us." With one hand she brought a slim dagger from her belt. "I've a mind to carve my name across the back the Spaniard lashed, to teach you manners, you sorry jackanapes! Just because I'm a woman, don't think I can't stand up for the honor of the coast brethren!"

She pricked him with the point of her dagger. Her eyes were bright and hard, and her mouth was twisted to one side of her face. The touch of that dagger was tinder to the fury that had been rising in Martin Chandos. He twisted sideways and the great bulk of his right arm rose and flung her a dozen feet. She went down on the bare wooden planks with a thump that shook the cabin.

And then she was snarling and lifting the dagger and hurling herself at him.

"No man raises his hand to Lizzie Hollister! I'll do more than carve my name in your skin! I'll write your epitaph under it!"

Against the pain that ate in him, Martin Chandos turned and put out his hands. He caught her wrists and swung her off her feet, so that she came toppling down on him in the narrow bunk. He locked a leg across the backs of her knees.

He found that he had caught a wildcat. For one moment he felt the softness of her flesh against his, and then she was clawing at him, dropping her dagger to rip at his face, flinging herself back and sideways against his legs and clutching fingers. Her breath came quickly, and Martin Chandos found it strangely sweet.

He was weak from shock and loss of blood. He held her for a moment, but there was the strength of a sleek tigress in her. Her fingernails raked his cheeks and her white teeth drew blood from his shoulder, and then she was off him and standing by the bunk.

Lizzie Hollister stared with wide eyes at the crimson gashes in his cheeks. There was anger in her, and a confused, frightening hunger.

"I ought to finish the job the Spaniard began! Or maybe you'd prefer some of the Exterminator's treatment? He'd slit your belly, nail part of your guts to a mast, and make you dance down the deck until your insides were laid out on its planks. Is that what you want me to do to you?"

His head rolled on the blankets spread across the bunk. His cheeks were white, but his mouth was set in a grim smile.

"Fash, do what you want! I've lost everything else. Why should I balk at giving up my life?"

She glared at him, arms rigid at her sides. She swung around and crossed the flooring under the hand-hewed beams from which ship's lanterns were suspended on creaking chains. Martin Chandos watched her walk away, and thought, It's a fair colleen she is, for all that she seems blood sister to the devil! If she were not the pirate wench he found her, she would be something to come to a man in his dreams.

She stood by the stern windows, with the dying sunlight coming in on her. "For a man whose back was whipped raw, you defend Spain hotly," she snarled.

"I'm not defending anyone, acushla. I say he was a damned pirate to board me when there's peace between our countries. And so he was!"

Her lips twisted as she slapped the carved woodwork of the bulkhead. "That is the way of Spain in the New World. Get used to it, if you're to stay here."

"Aye. Don Carlos gave me to understand as much. He's drawn an iron curtain across it, so he says. He means to keep everyone but Spanishers east of it."

"An iron curtain! I never thought of it like that, but it's true enough. A curtain formed of the ships and the steel of Spain. Penetrate that curtain, and you become fair game for her galleons. She'll take and sink you, and steal what you call your own. She'll kill and drag you off to slave in her labor camps, the mines. She's nothing but a robber!"

He grinned through the pain that was bringing big beads of sweat to his forehead. "Fash, mavourneen! Isn't that what I've been telling you?"

She swung around, and discovered that Martin Chandos was still and limp in the bunk. She came and stood over him, eying his thick chest and muscular arms. She put a brown hand to her heavy black hair and pushed it back over a shoulder. This Martin Chandos was not like the hairy, half-naked men who formed her crew, not like the vicious men she knew in Tortuga and Port Royal. There was something clean about him, like the air that swept from the Leeward Islands northwestward to Tortuga and beyond.

Her fingers lifted and traced the red scars that ran from his shoulders across his ribs and down to the curving hollow of his back. It was almost as if she caressed him.

Martin Chandos slept on, through the night and into the next day. At moments he would open his eyes dreamily, to stare at an empty cabin. He could feel the roll of the ship to the sea swells and hear the humming of the rigging as the wind lashed it. They were familiar sounds, and he slipped easily into the dreams from which a snapping sail or a sailor's cry had roused him.

There were times when he woke to feel the touch of fingers on his back, soft and gentle fingers that worked in soothing salves and ointments. Usually it was night, and the room was filled with black shadows and the pale flicker of a lantern's beams and a rich perfume that reminded him that it was a woman who knelt there.

At last there came a night when his eyes remained open, and his body was strong in the bunk, and he could feel the strength returning in him as he stretched the length of his body and yawned.

The sound of flowing water startled him and he turned his head. A woman was bent over a wooden washstand where an earthenware bowl had been set, lathering her face and upper body. A spill of black hair lay like a fan across her shoulders.

That Lizzie Hollister thought him asleep was obvious from the freedom with which she washed. A cloth soaked in suds was drawn from chin to the belt of her breeks. And then she was standing sideways to him, drying herself with a towel, and Martin Chandos choked back the cry that rose to his lips.

Her face was smooth and oval under the black froth of hair. Her mouth was full, ripe for kissing. The shoulders that she bared to the lantern light were smooth and golden. As if she felt his eyes on her, she swung about, the towel suspended. For a long moment she regarded him, and he lay motionless as a statue, wondering if she saw the glint of his slightly opened eyes.

And then Lizzie shrugged and resumed her toweling.

She moved beyond his vision, into the darker shadows, near an ornate lowboy. The sound of rustling cloth came to him, stirring him with its unknown mystery. He held his breath, waiting.

When Lizzie Hollister came out of the shadows, she wore a veil of black lace across her bosom, twisted up and knotted over one shoulder. A girdle of silver links supported a skirt of black silk. Her ball earrings and the thick ropes of brass balls around her neck clinked to her every step. She was barbaric and unashamed. She was something out of a man's dreams, pulse-stirring and exotic.

The woman went to the thick oak door and reassured herself that its iron bolt had been thrust home. She turned and stood in the beam of an overhead lantern, swaying a little as the ship rolled. Then she was moving to the bed, and there was a cadence in the swing of her shadowed hips and in the manner of her walk that sent a bolt of fire through the man on the bunk.

"Martin Chandos," she whispered, "you've been watching me for a long time. Open your eyes."

She stood beside the bunk, reaching out a hand to shake him. He lifted his lids and looked up at her. For once he could let the hunger that she roused show in his face, knowing it was expected. When she saw it, she laughed softly.

"I'm a far cry from any woman you've ever known, Martin Chandos! What tavern wench or merchant's daughter would so deck herself out for you?"

She spread her arms and went dancing across the worn rug on the cabin flooring. The lantern light went through the black silk of her skirt and played across her long legs.

He came up on an elbow, staring. Under the ship's lantern Lizzie Hollister whirled to a halt. On the table had been set a silver tray, covered by a snowy napkin. Her hand whisked the linen aside, and Martin Chandos saw a haunch of meat, two loaves of cassava bread, a bowl of green peas, and two mugs of steaming cocoa.

"Food for a hungry man," she mocked, meeting his hot eyes. "Come join me. Taste our cassava bread, mixed with red peppers. Try our lamantin, that is made from the flesh of the sea cow."

He swung his legs to the edge of the bunk until he felt the wooden floor under his bare feet. There was a ravening hunger in him, but it was mixed now with a different kind of hunger, as the red peppers were mixed with cassava flour. He stood erect, surprised by the fact that there was little weakness in him.

"You're as lovely as Deirdre herself, Lizzie darling! And as savage as Bricrin of the bitter tongue."

She watched him cross the floor in his worn homespun breeches. He was thinner than he had been when Redscar had hefted him over the starboard rail, but he was as big as ever, and the sight of his great chest and the long arms he had inherited from his Galway father made her catch her breath. This would be a rare night for Lizzie Hollister, in which she could repay some of the debts she owed men and their furious desires.

"Tonight you serve me as I served you," she told him. "You'll wait on me, and bring me food—and when I'm ready to use you, I'll do it, and not before!".

Their eyes locked. He smiled wryly, finding in himself a pity that softened his feelings toward her. He bowed and moved to the table. He lifted the platter that held the smoking lamantin and regarded her across the meat.

"It's a fine pirate lass you are, indeed! Fash, and it's true enough I'm your captive. So sit down and be waited on by a Chandos."

From under her long dusky lashes, Lizzie Hollister looked at him. Then she was striding freely across the cabin, to throw herself into a brocaded chair. Her hand beckoned him as she crossed one leg over the other.

He served her as she ate. He watched her seize a meat bone and gnaw at it with even white teeth. He watched her spoon peas and break the hard cassava loaf with strong fingers. There was a restlessness in Lizzie Hollister that was a tangible thing.

When she bade him, he sat at the table and fed himself, aware that her violet eyes were hard and bright. The food put new strength in him, and he found himself meeting her gaze with something akin to challenge. The ship surged on beneath the triangular sail at its lone mast, and the faint gurgle of her wake lifted above the counter and through the stern windows.

As he wiped his greasy fingers on a napkin, Lizzie Hollister leaned forward.

"You're a superior kind of by-blow, Martin Chandos. You take on the airs of a Versailles fop. You turn up your nose at buccaneers, but you fill your belly with the food they give you, and you didn't scorn to accept the salves I rubbed into your torn back."

She put a hand to a platter that was heavy with fruit, plucking a yellow banana from it. She began peeling it.

"What turns a man into a buccaneer, Martin Chandos? Ask yourself that question. These buccaneers used to be men as honest as yourself. Hunters of hogs and cattle they were, and butchers of flesh. They buccaned the meat over smoke fires, and sold it to passers-by, until Spain became aware of them. Then Spain decided to rid herself of these honest workingmen.

"In retaliation, these men struck back, in the only way they knew. If Spain wanted war, Spain would have war. They took to the sea in little ships, and attacked Spain's fine galleons. There's no law here in the West Indies but the law of force. There's no king to run to with a story of how you've been robbed. Peter le Grande showed them the way when he captured a Spanish galleon after sinking his own ship behind him, so he and his men had to win, or die!"

Not even in later years did it strike Martin Chandos as odd that he should sit here in a buccaneer cabin with a half-clad woman and listen to her discourse on the affairs of a world that knew a Sun King, Louis XIV of France, and a Charles II and his restoration program in England. A half-mad boy under the Queen Regent, María Ana, ruled Spain.

He said, "It isn't so much the fact you're buccaneers that bothers me, Lizzie darling, as it is the way you go about your business. By the snakes Saint Patrick drove from Ireland, instead of robbing a ship here and a ship there, you could band together and really teach those dogs of Spain a lesson!"

Her low laughter mocked him. "You'll be conceiving yourself as a man with a mission next. Come like a prophet to show us the way to run our trade!"

The laughter stung. He sat up straighter, and his blue eyes went hard. "It's not such a farfetched notion as you think. A man with brains and a little skill might do the trick. Like any greedyguts, Spain extends herself. Her holdings stretch from Cajamarca in Peru as far north as Matarmoros."

Lizzie put out a brown hand set with rings and lifted a succulent custard apple. Her black eyes gleamed smokily, as though an inner fire burned under the black lace vest she wore. White teeth flashed as she bit deep into the fruit.

"You sound like Harry Morgan. He has some such notion as yours. Hit Spain where it hurts the most. Teach her respect for the men she'd thrust like lepers from the Indies, and from this New World she considers her own. God love me! I've rescued a crusader!"

He stood up then, in his anger, and Lizzie Hollister let her gaze drift lazily over his chest and the wide sweep of his shoulders. He was a big man, powerful as a draft horse, yet lean and fit as a racer. Her lips thickened, and she discovered that the black lace across her shoulders was too tight.

"I was violated by a Spanish don, five feet from my mother on the deck of an English merchantman, when I first came out to the Indies!" she snarled. "That's what turned me to the sweet trade, Martin Chandos! Revenge on the men of Spain because of the foul dog who showed me what beasts men can be! And so, because I'm one of those buccaneers whom you affect to despise, I'll act like one!"

Her laughter, low and sensual, drifted through the little cabin like heady perfume. She stood, moving close to him. "But we've talked long enough. Crusader or man with a mission, you're my captive—mine, to do with as I want!"

There was flame in the eyes of Martin Chandos as he watched Lizzie Hollister sway before him. Her eyes and her laughter mocked him until he dragged her in against him with a wild cry.

Chapter Three

Martin Chandos woke to the thud of a distant saker. For a moment he lay bemused, turning to the woman beside him in the little bunk, her dark eyes open and sober, intent on his. The sun splashed through the stern windows, across the table and its silver service, touching the rug on the floor and the gilded bulkheads with yellow fingers.

Again the saker roared, and now Martin Chandos came out of the bunk to cross the stern cabin to its row of windows.

Out over the blue spill of tossing water he saw two tall red galleons under heavy sail, running free before the wind, bearing down on them. Below his feet he felt the surge of the Hussy as she crowded on more canvas, and the faint slap of feet that came from her deck as the buccaneers began uncovering deck cannons.

"Spaniards," muttered Lizzie Hollister. As her arm touched his, Martin Chandos could feel her tremble.

"They've come in answer to my prayers," he breathed softly. "Look at the fine, big build of them, Lizzie darling. Forty guns each, with sakers at her beak, and a clean spread of sail overhead. Ah, it's fine lessons we'll be after teaching them, acushla!"

Her black hair trembled as she shook her head, and now he could see the worry in her violet eyes. Her mouth, which had been so soft and warm last night, was tight with anxiety.

She muttered, "We're foul from being overlong at sea. And Raoul Sans Espoir, whose ship this is, is no clean mariner when he sails. I should have waited for my own ship, instead of renting his."

"A foul bottom! Fash, it's no more than I should have expected. If only those buckos abovedecks would stir their stumps to keep her shipshape, we wouldn't be at a disadvantage. But no matter! Get above, Lizzie, and take command."

"We've only twenty guns. Those ships have eighty between them."

He turned then and stared at her. "Why, so they have. The Forthright had only four. Four against sixty, and as true as Craftine played the harp at Tara, I almost took her. I would have done so, but a wave played me an unlucky trick."

"We'll let them come close, then board them!"

"Will you? If those dons are the seamen I think, they'll stand off and batter you to splinters. No, no, Lizzie. It's a sea fight that's ahead of us."

In her helplessness, Lizzie Hollister lost her temper. She whirled, and her eyes were violet pools of fury. "We can't run and we can't fight, you insufferable merchant!" she spat. "Now get out of my way while I go topside and consider our plight."

"Don't be too long considering, Lizzie darling, or the dons will have us five fathoms down, and still sinking. If you've no guts for a battle, I have! Move aside while I cover my skin!"

She tensed as if to launch herself at him, her fingers curved like claws. And then she shrugged and walked across the cabin to the screen where a big sea chest stood open.

They dressed in the silence of their secret thoughts. Martin Chandos crowded long legs into his dark brown breeches and sea boots of Cordovan leather. He found a white shirt freshly laundered and put it on. He had the thought, as he went up the companionway at Lizzie's heels, that he looked as much the buccaneer as any of the Hussy's crew.

The galleons were much nearer. He fancied that they had come up in the night, steering by the lanterns gleaming at the Hussy's stern, running free without their own lights showing to betray them. At dawn they were almost on their quarry. The geysers hurled up by their shots were only a hundred yards aft now. In a few moments they would be crashing into the poop, and splintering wood and metal.

The crew of the Hussy was grouped amidships, fronted by the giant Redscar. They were clad in shirts and breeks, with gaily colored sashes around their heads and middles. Their faces were the color of walnut from sun and sea spray, and barbaric earrings of gold and silver dangled from their ears.

Redscar lumbered forward. Two pistols were thrust into his wide leather belt, and a cutlass hung from the chains wrapped about his middle. His hairy chest was bare, and so were his feet beneath the jagged edge of his breeks. He lifted a hard, callused palm.

His eyes were bright as he said, "Even Montbars himself couldn't fight them two ships. Well, Lizzie? Do we beg quarter to stay alive for the privilege of sweating our guts out in some Peruvian silver mine?"

Lizzie Hollister had no chance to answer. It was Martin Chandos who stepped to the poop rail and put his big hands on its capping, staring down at the ragtail crew. His lips sneered.

"You call yourselves buccaneers? You'd let two Spaniards throw you in chains and work you to death in their mines? Faith, now, it's surprised I am. I always fancied you scum as fighting men!"

Redscar lifted his bush of crimson beard angrily. "Big words, merchantman! Words I'd take you up on, if it wasn't for them two yonder. I'm savin' my strength for when they board us."

It came to Martin Chandos as he stood on the poop deck, with two Spanish galleons at his back and threescore unwashed cutthroats below him, that sometimes a man has his luck thrust upon him by the whim of fate. He was an honest sea captain, but he had fought a ship under Penn, and later another under that unrecognized genius, Christopher Myngs. He had fought bigger odds and come out ahead. These men below were the finest sailors in the world. Knowing that, he found it easy to do what he must do.

He stabbed a finger at them. "Where's your sea anchor, you scum? Get me a man at the helm who knows what I want when I tell him! You others lay your nets against falling spars and rigging. I want gun crews at those ninepounders."

They gaped at him, jaws open. It was Redscar who waved an arm at the men behind him.

"Fall to, lads! What've we got to lose?"

Lizzie Hollister stood at his side. She asked savagely, "You think you can fight those ships? Twenty guns against eighty? With a foul bottom?"

His grin mocked her. "That's your fault, Lizzie acushla. Don't you ever careen and scrape her? How about your cannon? Will they shoot, or are they as foul as your keel boards?"

She opened her mouth to spit an answer at him, but he

pushed her aside and went to stand at the poop ladder. Under Redscar's bellowing voice, the crew was dragging out a rotted strip of canvas and spreading it. There were great ropes tied by knots at her corners.

"You call that a sea anchor, you lubbers?" he rasped. "I've seen better canvas on toy boats in Dublin town! Break out a sail and refit it. And mind, I want it done shipshape! Your lives will be depending on it."

There was authority in his voice. Despite themselves, the hairy men leaped to his bidding. Netting was strung against the rain of shell-splintered masts and rigging. Gun-port lids came open and linstocks were lighted. Muscles bulged under tanned skins as big black cannon balls were slung in canvas strips. At the helm, Redscar himself shouldered a man aside and swung the oaken whipstaff with a sweep of his powerful arm.

Slowly the Hussy swung to the tug of her sails as she came about. Now she was directly ahead of the nearer galleon, and coming abeam of it with such speed that a hoarse shout rose from the throats of the men crouched over their deck guns.

"You utter fool!" screamed Lizzie. "You've played right into their hands!"

While Redscar watched from the helm with feverish eyes, she hurled herself at him. One hand yanked at a long-barreled pistol that caught the sun as it came up. Martin Chandos went to meet her with a hard grin twisting his mouth.

"I know what it feels like to be helpless in the hands of those Spaniards, Lizzie acushla," he said, and caught her slim brown wrist in a big hand. "I won't fall into their clutches again, even for you!"

He twisted the wrist hard, and Lizzie screamed and went to her knees. The pistol fell and clattered across the deck planks. She was no weakling. Her free hand clawed at Martin's chest, ripping the cotton shirt, leaving four bleeding gashes from chest to navel. She leaned forward and her white teeth closed on the flesh at his middle, and his voice roared with the pain.

Martin Chandos' swung her up and held her high, dodging the feet she kicked at him.

"By the keel of Brendan's boat, you're a spitting wild-cat! But you're going to listen to sense if I have to stretch you out on the deck to make you listen. Not a man jack

in your crew can fight a ship. All they know is to creep
up behind it and swing grapples and go aboard. You
can't use those tactics here, you lovely hoyden!"

She squealed in her fury, her black hair swinging. Her
cheeks were flushed to the tint of old copper, and under
her black lashes her eyes were glowing violet coals.

"Redscar! Give me a hand with this thief! He's going
to steal my ship! Redscar!"

Martin Chandos turned her then and dropped her face
down over his left leg, bracing his foot on the binnacle.
He eyed her a moment, then grinned, and his big palm
dropped.

He spanked her there on the deck of the little bark as
it came about, and Redscar's angry bellow held the crew
to its tasks on the main deck and in the yards above.

And then Martin Chandos lifted her and dropped her
to the deck, looking down at the tears that streaked her
brown cheeks. She wept silently, like a wild thing, and
after a moment she crawled away to the taffrail, there to
stand and rub herself, and watch Martin Chandos with
eyes that were peculiarly bright.

He ignored her. He put his hands on the poop rail and
shouted, "Now, you unwashed scum of Tortuga! Test
your cannon on her!"

The captain of the nearer of the oncoming galleons,
the stately Claro de Luna, upon discovering that this rash
act of the fleeing buccaneer was seemingly delivering her
to his guns, made no attempt to shorten sail. He took no
thought of the motives of the Hussy's captain, other than
imagining that he had lost his reason in his fear. His own
red galleon was more than a match for this small buccaneer vessel, and on his starboard quarter his sister ship,
the Concepción, was straining her masts in an attempt to
be in on the fight.

And so the Claro de Luna came on with the wind, until her great golden beakhead faced the Hussy's larboard
guns.

Her broadside rocked the Hussy. Ten brass throats
roared, and smoke poured like a white mist across the
deck. It blinded everyone but Martin Chandos on the
poop. He roared at the giant Redscar, "Larboard your
helm, hard!" and turned back to the men who were
swabbing cannon breeches and reloading.

Now the buccaneers could see the wreckage of the

Claro de Luna's gilt beak, that carved and gilded wooden refulgence from which thrust the long bowsprit, the shattered ruin of foremast and knightheads. Her spritsail topmast lay across her forecastle and hampered the men who ran to clear the decks. She slowed in her run, veering slightly, and a cheer rose from the throats of the Hussy's larboard gun crew.

Slowly the Hussy swung about.

The galleon was now between the Hussy and her companion ship, the Concepción, thus sheltering the Hussy from the Concepción's guns. And as the Hussy slid slowly alongside the port side of the Claro de Luna, with her gun mouths gaping, her grim brown hull erupted again. This time the Hussy poured her shot high, in the manner of pirate ships, to smash the masts and rigging.

The Claro de Luna was too preoccupied with its shattered gear to answer that crushing broadside. Masts and sails drowned the gun crews on her deck. Men struggled under the weight of ropes and canvas, or screamed against the agony of broken bones. And as the galleon moved on ahead, another broadside, aimed lower, caught the men at the gun rails and blew them backward into a bloody welter.

The Hussy came sliding out of the fog of gunsmoke that wreathed her, moving to windward of the stricken Claro de Luna.

Martin Chandos growled down at Redscar, "Larboard your helm again, man, and order your best gunner to be after smashing that galleon's rudder!"

Redscar showed his teeth. His voice roared across the inferno of shouting, cheering men, and brought them back to a semblance of order. They ran to swab a Long Tom, reload, and light their matches. It took them three balls, but they smashed the rudder into an exploding fury of flying wood and metal.

As the Claro de Luna swung aimlessly to the swell of the waves, the Concepción came tacking about on a weather helm, circling to starboard, moving in a northwesterly course away from the crippled galleon. She bore down close-hauled on the Hussy. In a moment she would be directly ahead, with her own broadside ready to do to the Hussy what the Hussy had done to the Claro de Luna.

The men on the decks of the buccaneer ship groaned

and swore, but Redscar only grinned and waited, with the whipstaff in his fingers, for the orders of this magician on the poop deck.

"That sea anchor! Is she ready?"

"All ready, sir!"

"Then overside with her!"

The great sheet of white canvas bellied and shook as the wind took it. A cresting blue wave lifted and filled it, and it sank with a hum of the ropes that held it taut. Beneath the waves the canvas claw took hold, and it was as if some giant hand clasped the barnacled keel of the Hussy. She slowed to a halt in her forward run, and now the Concepción seemed to hurtle forward, her own speed increased in proportion to the sudden slowness of the Hussy.

The Concepción loosed its starboard guns, but the distance between the ships was now too great, for the sea anchor held the Hussy back as the Concepción sped by, dead ahead. One ball splintered a section of the forerail before it splashed overside, but the other balls were yards shy of their target.

A cutlass flashed in the sun, and the sea anchor fell away.

The Hussy jumped forward as if pushed. She came down astern of the Concepción as that great galleon frantically attempted to pay off. She caught the big red ship with a broadside in her stern from her starboard guns. The rudder and sternpost blew up amid a showering rain of glass from shattered stern cabins that were ornate with the gilded carvings of nymphs and cherubs. Like her sister ship, the Concepción drifted helplessly to the wind and waves.

She was useless after that. The Hussy swooped in on the wind and her larboard guns clawed the sails from her masts. She came back against the wind and her starboard cannon raked the Spaniard's decks.

In an hour it was over.

The two red galleons drifted with the waves as the Hussy sent out her boarding parties. Redscar came up from the helm to stand on the poop deck with Martin Chandos. There were devils in his hot black eyes.

"You'm a miracle man, sir! Nobody else on the Caribbee could o' done it. You'll be joinin' us now, of course."

Martin Chandos grinned. "Fash, it's the black sheep

of the family I am, true enough, born with a wandering foot and a roving eye. But I've no bent for a pirate's life."

Redscar eyed him warily. This big Irishman was strangely gifted in his understanding of a ship. He asked suddenly, "How did you do it? I saw it happening under my eyes, but damn them if I understood it!"

"The Little People came and sat on my shoulders and whispered in my ears," the Irishman laughed.

Redscar Hudson was a stolid Hollander, without the sensitive imagination that his Killarney mother had bestowed on Martin Chandos. He shrugged his puzzlement.

Martin Chandos went on. "They caught me out in a haystack with my mother's waiting maid when I was still in my teens, and they shipped me off to sea with Admiral William Penn. I found myself liking the sea and its clean winds and salty tastes. Before I went back to Galway, I commanded a frigate under Christopher Myngs."

Redscar growled, "I never knew an Irisher that was a sailor before."

"Are you telling me that you've never heard of the blessed Brendan?"

Redscar grinned. "Irishman or not, you've got a way with a ship under sail and with the guns it carries."

"I can fight a ship well enough, but as I say, I've no talent for your game."

Redscar shook his head until the rings in his ears flashed yellow with sunlight. His teeth were as white as pearls. "You'm think you bean't cut out for it, sir, but you are. You'm better'n Sans Espoir and Roc Brasiliano and even Harry himself at fightin' a ship! Redscar knows. I've fought with all of 'em, one time or the other."

They were interrupted by a great roar from across the water. A line of half-naked cutthroats was pressed to the starboard rail of the Concepción. When he made out the fevered cries, Redscar clapped a hairy paw to Chandos' shoulder.

"What'm I been telling you, sir? That you'm be cut out for a pirate? By the toes on my uncle's feet! You not only fight a ship like nobody else—you'm got the luck of Morgan, too! That be a plate ship!"

The power that Spain lost in the Old World when Drake and Frobisher crushed her Armada off the coast of England was not reflected here in the Indies. She owned silver mines in Peru, and her gilded galleons carried gold from her great ports at Cartagena and Panama. When the gold and the silver was gathered, the mighty ships that flew the lion of Spain fetched it eastward to Cadiz and Seville.

"It's one of those platers we've had the luck to smash!" howled Redscar, and his greed was a thing alive in him as he clung to the rail and shouted gleeful obscenities across the waves to his mates on the Concepción.

Lizzie Hollister swung forward from the station at the taffrail that she had adopted to watch this sea battle. She stood with the wind painting her thin shirt against her, breathing deeply of the tangy air.

"Redscar's right," she whispered. "You're one of us now. Those men will follow you to hell, if you'll only stand on the poop and give them orders."

He grinned at her. "Fash, if that's my destination, I won't be needing them to take me there. How's the backside I had to spank?"

Black hair swirled as Lizzie threw up her head. "I'll pay you back for that, Martin Chandos! But that's between the two of us. It doesn't concern your being a buccaneer."

"I'll be no damned pirate to please them or you. Put me down at St. Kitts. It's all I ask."

Her eyes glowed as they looked into his. There was a queer smile wrenching her full mouth. Her shoulder shrugged. "I couldn't do it if I wanted. They wouldn't let me. They've latched onto something big in you, Martin Chandos. You'll be a pirate, whether you will or not."

Beside him, Redscar turned his head, and his great earrings glittered as he nodded agreement. "The lads'll be taking a fancy to you after this. You've made us all rich, Martin Chandos! You pulled the Hussy out of an eighty-gun trap! Twenty guns against eighty! My uncle's nails!"

Something in Martin Chandos came alive as he stood at the poop rail and watched the Hussy's tender come bobbing back across the surging blue waters from the Concepción again and again, its thwarts buried under massive sea chests. They hauled those chests to the main deck, and dumped their golden contents out onto the wet wooden planks.

There were small gold boxes overspilling with rosy pearls and with rubies that were like hard red fire. Bars of Peruvian silver and ingots of raw yellow gold stood edge to edge in great mounds beside heavy statues of Inca kings carved in solid gold. Chains of thick gold coiled in heaps behind small mounds of diamonds from somewhere in the Guiana country.

Here a golden plaque was set with jewels, and there a round gold shield sparkled with the green glow of emeralds. Ropes of pearls like white grapes and bands of sapphires set in delicate golden filigree work were passed among hands that had already hefted and adjudged diamond-studded crosses and daggers. Other men knelt in a sea of golden ducats and doubloons, or tossed yellow guineas high.

Martin Chandos stood with Lizzie Hollister and Redscar Hudson and stared at more wealth than he had seen since Christopher Myngs had looted Coro.

"It fair turns a man's head," he whispered to himself, but the big Dutchman heard him.

"A captain's share for you, Martin Chandos! It was you who gave this to us. I'd guess near a hundred thousand pieces! Now what do you say to being a buccaneer captain?"

It was a temptation. With the sea wind playing in his long brown hair and across the ridged muscles of his wide back, Martin Chandos admitted that to himself. His tool cargo would have fetched only a thousand pieces, at best. His share in this treasure would make him rich for life. But he shook his head, and braced himself against the thing inside him that mocked at his scruples.

"Faith," he answered glumly, "you take a man and you twist his honesty with such a sight and with the fair words you speak. I thank you all, but I've got to answer no."

A deep-chested gunner shouldered a path between his mates. With a respectful knuckle at his forehead he growled, "Beggin' the Captain's pardon, but it's too late to say aught but aye. Them hidalgos know you were commanding the Hussy. They ain't ones to forget. You'll not be safe anywhere on the Main but at Tortuga or Port Royal."

A roar rose from the crew. They crowded in, dirty and bloody, begrimed with gunpowder and spray. Their laughter was hot and rousing, and the smell of salt air was in his nostrils, and gold and silver and precious jewels lay at his booted feet. There was no argument these men would listen to in this mood, or at this moment. Their compliments were fervid, and the thing that was deep in Martin Chandos clawed itself up from some buried corner of his being and gibbered at him.

He swung on them and spread his hands. "Now damn your eyes that see something in me I didn't know existed!"

He faced them across the treasure and he told himself, I could use my share to fight Spain in these waters! Don Carlos had spoken of an iron curtain of shot and shell that Spain was erecting. He could tear it down, with ships like those two red galleons rolling yonder in the heaving waves.

"I'll be your captain, if it's your wish. But at sea, my word is law. Obey me, and I'll make every unwashed man jack of you rich beyond his dreams!"

They sent a rolling shout out across the waters toward the tenders of the Concepción and the Claro de Luna, filled now with Spanish soldiery and sailors, pulling for Santiago de Cuba.

Then Martin Chandos sat on a gun mount and watched Redscar Hudson divide the spoils according to the articles that each man signed when he called himself a member of this grim brotherhood. He watched prize crews swung overboard to repair the great red galleons, and to refit them with spare masts and new rigging.

The buccaneers obeyed the Dutchman promptly. An understanding was coming to Martin Chandos, who was used to the grim service aboard a warship, with the life or death of every hand at the mercy of the captain's whim or mood, that these men worked in a perfect democracy, a democracy of obedience to leadership when they saw for themselves that such leadership was good.

He ate that night in the stern cabin with Lizzie Hollister.

He treated the rich Malaga wine with care, but it was powerful and heady, and he found himself eying Lizzie with clearer vision. His eyes went again and again to the silk of her shirt. Once, as she leaned to tear a haunch of beef from the stew on its silver platter, she caught his eyes on her and laughed.

"You've won over the men, Martin Chandos, but there's still Sans Espoir to reckon with. It's his ship I rented and his men you fought with today. Aye, and his woman you had in your cabin last night! He'll be in Tortuga to demand an accounting of you. He'll imagine that the share the lads voted to you belongs to him."

She wiped her fingers on a napkin. Her eyes were bold and hot under their long black lashes. He read the challenge in them. His big hand went out and closed on her wrist. He dragged her like that from her chair, and down across his lap.

He grinned into her flushed face. "We might as well give him something to account for, then!"

She tried to fight, but he was too strong for her. His mouth trailed kisses across her neck and upward to her lips. She shivered at the touch of his fingers. "You're a devil straight from hell, Martin Chandos!"

Her hair hung back and brushed the arm of his chair as he doubled her arms and brought them down behind her back. He laughed gently, watching her eyes.

"Sure, it's the devil I am with a ship and with a woman! Isn't that so, Lizzie darling?"

She struggled with him, but a big hand prisoned her wrists as he grinned into her flushed face.

"It's a real woman you are, by the wisdom of Bridget herself! I'd forgotten how much of a woman, with that fight with the Spaniards and the sight of all that gold spilled across the deck planks on my mind."

She squirmed and cursed him, but his laughter warmed her, and the curses died on her lips.

Chapter Four

THE ISLAND OF TORTUGA lay northwestward of Hispaniola, in latitude 20.30'. Its great bulk towered high and round like the back of the turtle after which it was named, the green fronds of its candlewood and china-root trees seeming like moss on its rocky shell. The azure waters of the Caribbean lapped at the white coral sands rimming its shores, and beyond them, towering into the green immensity of its jungles, rose the great fortress of La Tour, which Bertrand d'Ogeron had built in the name of the French West India Company, to replace the Fort du Rocher constructed by Lavasseur and burned by the Spaniards a little over a decade before. A number of thatch-roofed huts stood between the shore and the high bluffs, and here and there a more pretentious house lifted its white walls. Nestled between the high sheer bluffs of black rock, enclosed as if by the hands of some great giant, was the landlocked bay called Cayona.

Martin Chandos stood on the quarter-deck of the Hussy as it ran through the shallow channel behind the red bulks of the captured Concepción and Claro de Luna. The blue waters of the bay were littered with small barks and ketches, *pataches* and brigantines. These were the ships of the buccaneers who were not at sea, but resting in the taverns and inns that ranged behind the huge bulk of the Mole, along the Rue du Quai. His seaman's eye went over them, judging them for their seaworthiness.

Redscar Hudson lumbered to stand beside him. His teeth were bared in a grin. "They're not the kind of ships you want, Chandos. You want big ones, like the two red beauties we took from the dons. Four or five of yon galleons, filled with the members of the brotherhood, and you could walk into Cartagena itself."

"It's what I was thinking," admitted the Irishman. "With enough of those ships, we could challenge a plate fleet."

The big Dutchman licked his lips at that thought, and they parted, Redscar Hudson to supervise the unloading of the sea chests, Martin Chandos to pace the quarter-deck of the Hussy from binnacle to forerail. He told himself that he was an honest seaman, wanting no part of this "sweet trade," desiring only that his stolen cargo and crew be restored to him. But as he breathed in the hot salt air and stared at the bulk of the great walled fort high on Tortuga's mountainside, he admitted to himself that something was aborning within him. He was conceiving visions of empire.

With a fleet of forty-gun galleons, he thought, and a crew to sail and fight them, I could harry Spain from one end of the Caribbean to the other! I'd claw down her iron curtain. Aye, and bring men and women from Dublin town, from London and Paris, to build new lives in this new land!

The creaking of the capstan bars as the Hussy's anchor went splashing overside in three fathoms of blue water recalled him to the moment. His lips twisted in a grim smile. Thus far, his vision was only an idea in his head.

I've got a lot to do yet to make it come true, he admitted. He counseled himself that it might be well to meet this Bertrand d'Ogeron, who was governor of Tortuga, with a trace of caution, though his Irish blood whispered to him to be as bold before him as Shane the Proud had been at Armagh. While he was in this mood, Lizzie Hollister found him bent over the rail, brooding at the whitewalled houses roofed with palmetto leaves that swung in an arc from the ruins of Fort du Rocher to La Tour.

Lizzie wore a clean shirt and freshly laundered breeks above her red sea boots. Her lack of pistols and cutlass was a concession to the fact that her ship was anchored in home waters. The brass earrings and necklaces had been polished, and Martin Chandos could detect a trace of perfume in the thick black hair that was gathered by a bow at the nape of her neck.

"You'll go ashore with me?" she asked. "I'll take you to the Governor. You'll find him a courteous man, Martin, but don't anger him by deriding his buccaneers. They offer money and protection in these waters to France."

Martin Chandos shrugged. "I'll be keeping a civil tongue in my head, if that's what you mean."

They went overside to a cockboat manned by half a dozen pirates, whose powerful muscles soon had the cockboat's bow bumping against the pilings of the Cayona wharf. From the Mole to the Rue du Quai was but a few steps. From there to the mansion that housed Bertrand d'Ogeron was a fair walk, between the taverns and the little shops that flanked the coral-sand street, glittering whitely under the tropic sun.

Heat lay like a smothering veil across the island. Dogs sprawled in tongue-lolling abandonment in the shade of overhangs, and in this noonday swelter even the taverns were quiet. Two women in cloth dresses, their heads bound in the high colorful turbans peculiar to the Indies, swept by in an aura of cheap perfume. In the distance they could see the palmetto trees that fringed the white length of the Governor's mansion.

M. Bertrand d'Ogeron served the West India Company of France. He was a man of medium height who affected the manners and the rich garb of Europe even in the stifling sultriness of these lands. His periwig was a masterpiece of curling black hair reaching to his shoulders, and the rich long coat that was trimmed with yellow ribbons was a background to the fashionable shoulder belt of thick brocade that fell to his loose breeches, bedecked with yards of thick lace.

He stood now before a rosewood cabinet as Martin Chandos and Lizzie Hollister came into the darkness of the library, whose jalousies were drawn against the sun. For a moment, as their eyes grew accustomed to this darkness after the blaze of the sunlight, they did not see the man who sat on the edge of the chair, scowling blackly.

It was Lizzie who recognized him, and started forward. "Raoul! I thought you off the coast of Cuba!"

"*Tiens!* That's where I was, before a black Spaniard sought me out and hammered me to splinters. He was tall and lean and he laughed like the devil. *Corbleu,* his ship was fast! Fast and big, with sixty guns, and a great gold cross on her beak that—"

Martin Chandos hit his fist against the top of a refectory table of black walnut. "The same! The same damned pirate that stole my ship and crew, and whipped my back to shreds!"

Raoul Sans Espoir turned his regard from Lizzie Hollister. His eyes were brown in a heavily tanned face, and his thin, cold lips were twisted. He asked harshly, "Who is he?"

Raoul Sans Espoir was a native of Languedoc, and he had come west across the Atlantic as cabin boy for the Chevalier de Fontenay, whose fleet wrested Tortuga from the murderers of Lavasseur and restored it to the French crown. Liking this high-cliffed island, seeing in these sea rovers a chance to win fortune, he had elected to stay on. His initial successes against unarmed treasure ships had given him a confidence equaled only by his arrogance. He considered himself a Gallicised Henry Morgan.

Lizzie Hollister made explanations of a sort, and Martin Chandos noted that she left out all mention of the role he had played with her in the stern cabin. Sans Espoir broke in on her recital, to which Bertrand d'Ogeron listened with rapt attention, as she was relating how he fought the Hussy's twenty guns against the Spaniards' eighty.

The Frenchman scowled haughtily. "He named the man who shot the Sorcière out from under my feet a 'damned pirate,' I think. I'm such a 'damned pirate' myself. The man who sunk me was not. So I'm a liar and a damned pirate all in the same breath. It calls for satisfaction!"

"Raoul!" cried Lizzie.

Sans Espoir brushed her aside with an arm and moved toward Martin Chandos. His thin lips smiled cruelly. He was spare and tall, with a willowy grace that belied the strength of his muscles. At the moment, shame and rage worked in his veins at the loss of his ship, a shame and a rage that had been nurtured by the forty-three-league row he and his men had made in bobbing longboats to Tortuga.

Raoul Sans Espoir lifted a hand to bring its palm across the face of the man before him. Instead, his wrist was caught and held in a grip like an oaken vise.

Martin Chandos smiled. "Ah, no, m'sieu! I've had my back marked by a Spaniard already. I wouldn't relish the same treatment on my cheek from a Frenchman."

Sans Espoir hissed, "Release me, you Irish swine! Loose your fingers or I'll put a ball between your ribs!" He was reaching for the curved butt of his pistol when Bertrand d'Ogeron shook his arm, even as Lizzie Hollister tugged at the brocaded coat with which he aped the garb of the Governor.

"If you please, m'sieu!" snapped d'Ogeron. "He is my guest. You must not violate the laws of Tortuga. There shall be no killing within my walls. What you choose to do in the town below is another matter."

The Frenchman drew back, his lips curving in a tight

smile. He bowed stiffly to the Governor. "I beg your for-
giveness, m'sieu," he said softly to d'Ogeron. "My late
tribulations caused my temper to explode. It will not do
so again. Come, Lizzie. Your arm!"

Lizzie Hollister looked back over her left shoulder as
she swaggered toward the door with the French buccaneer. Her dark eyes were hot and triumphant. Martin
Chandos found himself wondering about the rage into
which her description of his more intimate activities
aboard the Hussy would throw Raoul Sans Espoir when
she told him.

His musings were interrupted by the Governor of Tortuga, who regarded him down the length of his thin,
patrician nose. "Well, sir? I gathered from what Lizzie
said that you're a merchant captain out of Plymouth. It
appears that you labor under a misapprehension as to
the identity of your assailant."

"I'm under no misapprehension!" Martin Chandos exploded. "He was a Spaniard, and a damned pirate as
well!" He went on in his description of the lean man who
had stood and laughed as a cat-o'-nine-tails cut his back to
red ribbons.

When he was done, the Governor lifted out a silver
snuffbox and indulged his nostrils with two pinches of
the brown stuff. His generous mouth was smiling as he
waved a wrist wreathed in Bruges lace. "Be seated, sir.
Allow me to further the explanations that Lizzie Hollister and Redscar Hudson have given you. Spain is held
back from ownership of these rich lands only by the men
who live in the town of Cayona, through which you
passed as you climbed to my home. Those men were
peaceful butchers—butchers of the flesh of wild cow and
boar that roam the hills of Hispaniola—at a time not so
long ago. With their muskets and their companions, they
lived a wild, free life, bothering no one. Then Spain sent
an expedition to destroy them."

Bertrand d'Ogeron paused in his pacing before the
great brick fireplace to proffer his guest a silver platter
piled high with mammee apples. He went on, after replac-
ing the platter. "As is usually the case when we interfere
with something that causes us no concern, Spain stirred
up a hornet's nest. Turned away from their peaceful pursuits, these buccan traders turned to the sea. In little
ships they struck back at Spain, once their eyes had been

opened by a Frenchman from Dieppe named Pierre le Grande. He showed the way. The others followed.

"Today, M'sieu Chandos, your pirates are buccaneers —driven from their hunting and meat-curing pursuits by this Spain they now hunt on the Caribbean. And as buccaneers, they maintain a balance of power here between England, who is too poor to furnish fleets of ships for protection, France, who is not willing, and Spain, who has the money and the ships and the greed to hurl all but herself out of these West Indian waters."

Martin Chandos smiled grimly. "Something of all that I already understand. My only complaint is with the methods of your buccaneers. They steal up and board a ship and make themselves no better than sea robbers."

D'Ogeron lifted his brows and spread his white, carefully tended hands. "They regard their activities as a trading venture, sir. They risk their lives against Spanish gold."

"With enough ships, they could sweep Spain out of these waters. They could open up the West Indies to England and France, to people who could come from the crowded Old World to fine, new homes in the new one."

The Governor laughed softly. "You ask them to be altruists, to risk their lives for men and women they don't know?"

Martin Chandos went to stand at a jalousied window from which, over the palmetto gardens that fringed a patio on the westward side of the mansion, he could look down at the sprawling whiteness of the town.

"I'll pay them well for those risks. Give me ships and enough men, and I'll take Panama and Cartagena. I'll fly the black flag over those cities. I'll tear them from Spanish hands and give them into the hands of people who won't be English or French or Dutch or Spanish, but a new breed. A breed of men born in the Americas. A mixed breed of all nations. A fine, new race of men with no ties to the Old World but those of sentiment."

Bertrand d'Ogeron laughed. "Even Harry Morgan dares not dream so much. All he seeks is gold. You seek land and a new way of life."

"By the Killarney blood in my mother's veins, someday that dream will be a reality."

"Perhaps, perhaps. But for the moment, let us discuss the ways and means of disposing of your fortune. It has been my habit, when dealing with the buccaneer captains of Tortuga, to find a market for their wares in Basse-Terre. For some I deposit letters of credit in France. To others I give cash, cash that they soon spend on drunken trollops in the taverns down below."

Martin Chandos shook his head. "I want ships. Ships and men. Get me the Claro de Luna. Redscar Hudson will find me the men. I'll seek out Don Carlos on the sea he conceives to belong to Spain, and rip down the iron curtain he boasts of constructing. And in doing that, I'll help found that new land for that new breed of men I've been imagining."

Bertrand d'Ogeron put his head to one side and surveyed this big Irishman who talked like a mad prophet. He said softly, "You will be a most unusual buccaneer, Martin Chandos. I am very eager to learn how you will make out in your crusade."

Martin Chandos put his hand on a thick brocade drape and tightened his fingers until that hand became a fist. "One thing more. The crew that Don Carlos took off my ship—what will he do with them?"

"Work them to death, in the mines of Castillo del Oro."

"I thought as much. I'll make a vow now, so I will, to free them from their slavery! Before I'm done, I'll strike their manacles from their wrists with my own hands!"

The Governor of Tortuga took another pinch of snuff. "A most laudable vow, m'sieu. One I hope you live to fulfill. But you'll excuse my doubts on the matter. Even Harry Morgan admits Panama is too well defended to be attacked."

"Someday I must meet this Harry Morgan. But until then, see to my moneys, and arrange for me to purchase one of the red galleons Lizzie Hollister and I brought to Cayona Bay."

He was turning when a footfall sounded in the hall. A woman came to the door and stood there, a woman with yellow hair so pale it was almost white, and a skin that was smooth and creamy above the boned bodice of scarlet satin adorned with tiny white bows. On her cheek and at the corner of her vivid red mouth she wore black beauty patches. Her dark blue eyes, surveying him shamelessly, were bold and haughty.

She was a woman out of the extravagant court of Louis

XIV, and her scarlet gown was heavy with silver lacing, her elbow cuffs supporting a foot-long spray of Mechlin lace. For a moment she paused to examine him, and then her wide red mouth curved flirtatiously.

"*Ma foi!* A new face! *Chéri,* come see!"

It was then that Martin Chandos discovered the tall, slender youth behind the woman. He was a brooding, serious man with black eyes in deepset sockets and a wide, swart forehead under the glossy black periwig he affected. His short jacket of red satin revealed a lingerie shirt thick with Quesney lace, and the tubular breeches on his legs were decked with a froth of *galants* loops. His shoes boasted high red heels, and the stockings above them, reaching to the breeches, were clocked in cloth of gold. His sullen face, dark and somber, belied this ornate garb, which Martin Chandos was later to discover to be a protestation against the poverty of his family.

The man said slowly, "You will enjoy that, Céleste. A new face to occupy your eyes." The black eyes lingered on Martin Chandos' bulk almost angrily, and the Irishman fancied he could read jealousy in those black depths.

Bertrand d'Ogeron moved forward into the little pause. He said brusquely, "God knows there are few enough faces in Tortuga worth a girl's study these days. Céleste, this is Martin Chandos, a newcomer from Ireland. M'sieu Chandos, my daughter, Céleste. The gentleman at her elbow is Pierre Lelande, Vicomte de Piercy."

The Irishman smiled, bowing. He studied the faces before him, seeing rebellion and bitterness on the swart features of the Vicomte, anger and resentment puffing the cheeks of the Governor. Only the woman was at ease, and it came to Martin Chandos that her ease was only a mask she wore to stifle the fear in her heart.

Admiring her spirit, he regarded her more closely. She was a breath of the Old World here in the New World. Her troubled blue eyes held his a moment, the fear in them changing slowly to defiance.

The Vicomte de Piercy was muttering, "Come, Céleste. We have not yet begun our walk."

Bertrand d'Ogeron said harshly, "*Mais non!* Too long have you usurped my daughter. Permit her a little time with my guest. Céleste, show M'sieu Chandos the garden."

Céleste laughed and spread her white hands. The defiance was stronger in her now as she tilted her white chin at him. "You are aware, m'sieu, that daughters have no wills where their fathers command."

She put her hand to his forearm, and looked back at the glowering Vicomte. "I will see you tomorrow, Pierre. *Au revoir.*"

"I do not favor the role of kidnaper, ma'mselle," the Irishman told her as she guided him to the large, glass-paned doors that were open to the flagstoned patio. "If you would prefer to remain within doors . . ."

She smiled at him. "It will do M'sieu le Vicomte good to brood a little over me. Lately he becomes too certain of my company."

"A trait I'd regard with envy," he told her.

His words brought her sober blue eyes up to dwell on his a long moment. It seemed to the Irishman that she was looking at him as a man for the first time, and the sensation was not unpleasant.

The mansion gardens lay west of the house, out of sight of the town and the curving beach. Here Bertrand d'Ogeron had set stone flagging and marble benches bordered by rows of flowering cannas in red and yellow, with the frail purple blooms of lush orchids blossoming below the tall stateliness of royal palms. As he walked, Martin Chandos began to imagine the golden girl as the fairest flower in the entire garden.

Her smile was secretive as she came to a stop beside a chinawood fence. "I saw you watching us in the library. You are an observant man, m'sieu. You will have noted that the Vicomte and Papa are not the most amiable of friends."

He shrugged. "I've seen more antagonistic relationships dissolved with time."

Céleste d'Ogeron swung around at that, and now the mobile lips were laughing, and there was a new brightness in her blue eyes. "Have you truly? Ah, that would be fine!" It was as if a mood had dropped from her like a cloak whose clasp she loosed. She became gay, talkative. Her white hands gestured at the jungle beyond the house and at the beach below. She gave him a little of the history of this Turtle Island and of the turn of events that had brought her father to succeed Lavasseur.

For his own part, Martin Chandos discovered that it was easy to laugh with this girl in the tropic sunshine. The perfume of her pale yellow locks and the sight of

her strong white shoulders and wide red mouth were like
strong wine, and her courtly speech and soft laughter became a melody in his ears. He bent above her as she sat
on a marble bench under a scarlet bougainvillea, and
told her something of his early youth, and of the family
that had packed him off to sea. Under the encouragement
of her blue eyes, Martin Chandos became garrulous. He
was discovering in this pale beauty an echo of his youth.
He was seeing in her the gracious Irish noblewomen who
strolled the parks of Belfast and Dublin, or who had gone
overseas with the Earl of Tyrone in his banishment.

It was, for him, a moment of relaxation from the nightmare of piracy in which he found himself; and in that
relaxation, his eyes were opened to the proud loveliness
of this French girl, and the standard of nobility that she
represented.

For her part, Céleste d'Ogeron found in this big Irish
adventurer a welcome relief from the gloomy possessive-
ness of the Vicomte de Piercy. It was fun to flirt and
laugh again, and feel male eyes roving over her shoulders.

It was with surprise that Martin Chandos discovered
the sun to be low in the west. He straightened, exclaim-
ing, "Fash! I'd no idea I'd kidnaped you for such a long
time. Believe me, the captor enjoyed the imprisonment,
even if the prisoner didn't."

She laughed and tapped his chin with her fingertips.
"You fish for compliments, m'sieu. I did enjoy it. Every
moment of it. You are like a breath of spring air here in
my tight little home."

As he lifted her white hand to kiss it, her fingers
squeezed his warmly. Lifting his head, he saw her blue
eyes flirting with him. He took encouragement from that
look and from the pressure of her fingers.

With that encouragement buoying his steps, he moved
from the garden to the town that sprawled below.

Smoke drifted like marsh mist through the common
room of the Stag's Horn Tavern. Grimy beams reflected
the red light of a hundred brass oil lamps smoldering in
their iron brackets. A woman danced on dirty bare feet
in the wine pools that dotted a table's surface, as a score
of throats roared approval. A dozen seamen sat at a round
table in a corner of the room, toying with a deck of
lansquenet cards. Beyond them, at tables of guaiacum

wood, sat others of the brethren, drinking palmetto-juice wine or filling their drinking cans with oily rum. Here and there a man lay sprawled on the dirt floor, snoring drunkenly, and was paid no heed until one less gone in his cups stumbled over him.

At a narrow table placed close to a latticework of china-root, two men sat with their backs to the wall. Redscar Hudson was chuckling. "Ninety thousand pieces! All your own, Martin Chandos. The lads voted you equal shares with Lizzie."

"Your doing, you redheaded jackanapes!"

The big sailing master laughed softly and worked his palm down the length of the scar on his cheek. "I'll not deny my words carried some weight. The lads want you as captain, so I pointed out to 'em: What better way to make you one than to vote you a captain's share?" The red-bearded giant paused to heft his drinking can and empty it at a swallow. He drew a sleeve across his mouth and winked. "You want the Claro de Luna now, don't you? A good ship. Better nor her sister, the Concepción. Her bottom's been coated with pitch and chopped horse-hairs."

Martin Chandos smiled and moved the pewter drink-ing can around in a circle on the tabletop. "Her lines are not completely Spanish. The pitch and horsehairs are an English trick. It might be that the Claro de Luna is a captured galleon. From the cut of her hull, I'd judge her something Peter Pett might turn out of his yards."

Redscar Hudson banged his mug on the table planks. He roared, "Stab me easy! You're a devil to know that! The lads showed me stolen papers from the ship's log. I didn't know they'd told you."

"They didn't. It's only the eyes of me I used. Your Spanishers are usually too high in forecastle and stern. They're floating castles, most of them, and as clumsy in the water. But the Claro de Luna has trimmer lines and a more rounded stern. She'll carry close to sixty guns without harming her sailing grace."

Redscar nodded and put a sobering hand on his cap-tain's arm. He grunted, "See who comes yonder, like a wolf hunting its prey."

Raoul Sans Espoir strode slowly between the tables, arrogant and scowling, with his eyes fixed on the table where Martin Chandos sat with Redscar. He leaned on an ebony cane that matched the black satin of his brocaded greatcoat, and a cravat of white Spanish lace was fluffed across his chest. A feathered felt hat with a wide brim and low crown protruded downward across the long brown curls of his periwig.

As he halted before them he said, "I am informed you are due for congratulations, Martin Chandos. You fought my ship the Hussy with able seamanship. You took two prizes. The men voted you a captain's share of the merchandise. Since you've no inclination for the life of a damned pirate, I'll relieve you of the necessity. You'll turn the ninety thousand over to me."

Martin Chandos stretched his legs to one side of the table. His face was affable as he lifted it to look the better at the French buccaneer.

"Don't be after troubling yourself. Lizzie rented your ship, and paid you gold for her. It's only your jealousy that gives you a claim on our prize moneys."

The Frenchman fumbled in his sleeve. His eyes were hard as his lips writhed back from small, even teeth. "Ah? Then I'm to understand that you refuse to give me the moneys voted you?" His black eyes slid sideways toward Redscar Hudson, and that giant knew a moment when fear ran down his spine on icy legs.

"The moneys are mine. Legally voted me. I'll keep them. And one of the galleons I captured. Lizzie can have the other."

Raoul Sans Espoir swore, and brought his hand out of his sleeve.

There was a small pistol in the circle of his fingers. Redscar Hudson, who had thought he groped for a snuffbox, cried out harshly. The pistol came up and leveled.

Martin Chandos did not wait for the forefinger to tighten on the trigger. His extended legs rose, and as one foot locked around Raoul Sans Espoir's left ankle, the other shoved against his knee. Hooked off balance, the Frenchman went backward, his gun exploding to send its ball into a wooden beam, while he crashed on his back amid the slops and mud of the tavern floor.

Martin Chandos was like a cat. He went down on a knee and his big hands locked in the lace shirt and the brocaded front of the greatcoat. His muscles heaved and the Frenchman came off the floor, to be thrust backward over the table where Martin Chandos had been drinking.

"Well, now, Captain," said the Irishman softly, "what do I do with you? Choke you to death here in the Stag's Horn? Or let you live to murder me some other time?"

Raoul Sans Espoir was a cruel man, and like so many cruel men, he was a coward under his twisting lips and sneering eyes. He babbled, "M'sieu, forgive me! It was a joke, a jest to test you for the buccaneer life."

"He lies in his teeth," snarled Redscar. "Wrap your fingers around his throat and be done with him."

Martin Chandos stood up and brought the Frenchman with him. In his big hands he lifted him, holding him high above his head. Then, with a ripple of powerful muscles, he hurled him ten feet across the room, onto a table. The table spilled and rolled, scattering its cards and drinking cans, to the fervid swearings of a dozen voices.

The buccaneer captain lay stunned. Eyes turned from him to the man who had thrown him like a sack of cassava flour. Redscar Hudson rolled into the sudden silence, jerking a thumb over his shoulder.

"That's him I been telling you lads about. Him that saved the Hussy from eighty guns. Martin Chandos is the name, lads. A name you'll be hearing from now on. We took close to half a million off the Claro de Luna. Wi' pearls and other sundry jewels!"

The silence exploded into a babble of voices. Redscar winked back at Martin Chandos, and caught his arm in a hard grip. "Come along now, Captain. Leave the lads to talk over what happened among themselves. It'll give 'em food for thought."

That Martin Chandos had made an enemy in Raoul Sans Espoir he knew without being told. He found evidences of it as he walked through the narrow coral streets of Cayona next day, in the easy familiarity of grinning English and Dutch buccaneers, in the hard looks of some Frenchmen. But Tortuga was more melting pot than nation. Even those Frenchmen who looked hardest at him agreed that he was a good addition to the brotherhood, especially if he could repeat with some other ships what he had done with the Hussy. There was no argument so convincing with the brethren of the coast as the color of gold and the prospect of more to come.

And so Martin Chandos made his plans. In the cool dimness of the Governor's library he finished his nego-

tiations with Lizzie Hollister for the purchase of the
Claro de Luna. By the articles of agreement, his share of
the captured ships was almost equal to her own, and the
scratch of her quill pen across a length of parchment
made Martin Chandos captain of the Claro de Luna.

Lizzie Hollister left as soon as she had written her
name across the parchment that waived her rights in the
galleon. There was Canary to be sipped in silver cups,
and over the candied fruits Bertrand d'Ogeron became
eloquent as he put an official blessing on Martin Chandos.

"One ship now, Martin. Perhaps three later on. Then
five. In ten years, twenty. A formidable fleet."

"I'll take Cartagena and Puerto Bello long before that,"
the Irishman said. "You'd make an old man of me before
I put to sea!"

The Governor leaned forward, smiling slightly. His
eyes were keen and brilliant. "If I seem to do so, I only
point out the difficulties in your path. You play at em-
pire-building, Martin Chandos. You're better as a buccaneer."

Martin Chandos stood up and placed his silver cup
down very gently on the rosewood table. "You may be
right. I wouldn't know. There's only one way to learn,
and I mean to take it. No amount of your blather is
going to stop me, either."

Bertrand d'Ogeron was politely apologetic. He did not
want to be misunderstood. Always, he had the welfare of
his buccaneers at heart. True, they meant money in his
pocket, but that was incidental. He must first of all be
a good servant for the French West India Company.

Martin Chandos left by the harbor door. As he was
passing a clump of pimento trees, a voice called softly to
him. He whirled, aware that he now knew why he had
rummaged through the chests of the captured galleons
last night, to find a plum velvet coat and doublet with
petticoat breeches to match, and ribbed stockings of lavender silk. Great butterfly bows ornamented his modish
shoes. He was prepared now, clad as a grandee of Spain,
to meet this lovely woman who appeared to step straight
from the Sun King's court, in yellow satin and black lace.

Céleste d'Ogeron twirled a parasol over a shoulder as
she stood on the patio flagging and watched him ap-
proach. Her eyes lit at sight of his new elegance.

"You are a far cry from a buccaneer captain this morning, M'sieu Chandos. I find you quite the gentleman."

"You overwhelm me, ma'mselle. I can only explain that once I was captain of a frigate in service of the Protectorate. I learned some manners and modes in that time."

They walked between flaming hibiscus and tall, willowy poinciana trees. As they strolled, Martin Chandos discerned a trace of homesickness in the lovely woman in the yellow satin gown. She spoke of the hills of Languedoc and the gentle valley of the Loire, and of her girlhood on the Ogeron estates.

"For myself," he answered, "I find the green hills of this new world cleaner and fresher than those of the old. We dropped anchor in New Amsterdam once, and I went ashore. There were Indians in the streets, painted red savages, as colorful as—"

"Lizzie Hollister?" asked Céleste softly, her gaze slanted sideways toward him.

Martin Chandos flushed.

The Frenchwoman went on gently. "I understand you spanked her in full view of her crew."

He fancied he could read laughter in her dark blue eyes, but he assured himself he was mistaken. He stammered excuses, but her hand touched his warmly and she shook her head.

"No need for apologies, m'sieu. Even with that spanking, I envy little Miss Spitfire." At his surprised glance, she nodded, and now the laughter in her was gone. *"Oui,* envy! You find it so strange? She is free. She can come and go, meet whom she will, laugh when she wants and cry when and where she wants."

"I had not conceived you a prisoner," he murmured, watching her white chin, with its little black star of a beauty mark set close to her full red lips, as it lifted imperiously.

"You lack observation, then, M'sieu Chandos. I am as much a prisoner of my father, and the rules that govern the lives of gentle-born ladies, as though I were in the dungeons at Panama. What Papa says for me to do, I do. What Papa dictates that I wear, I wear. When he says laugh, I laugh. It is a puppet you see before you."

The Irishman knew the system that gave the father and husband of the family the power almost of life and death within his family. Sons and daughters married the brides and grooms selected for them. Everything on their backs was the property of the parent. It was a daring son who could cut loose the family ties; and thinking of that, he thought also that he was one of them. Perversely, the thought brought with it a hard, sick wrench of home-sickness that the sight of this young woman, in her Old World finery, did little to mitigate.

To bring a smile to her lips, he jested, "If I had the powers of Bricrui of the poisoned tongue, it's myself would challenge your father to a duel, that I might free you from those bonds."

Her blue eyes brooded at him. In their depths he fancied he read bitterness. She said, "You speak in jest, m'sieu. And yet so often the joking tongue is the truthful tongue."

He knew she spoke in allegory, and that what she had in mind was not a duel. As he pursued his thoughts still further, he grew thoughtful. There was a way to remove Céleste d'Ogeron from the imprisonment that chaffed her. Marriage with a man like himself would free her.

Telling himself that this was a notion that might take some meditation, he walked on a little more with her.

Guiltily he realized that he would be committing himself to the buccaneering life by remaining here at Tortuga. It was that same sense of guilt that made him appreciate the fact that marriage with this woman could put all that behind him. And yet her father consorted with these same buccaneers. The very clothes on her back had been purchased by gold that was Bertrand d'Ogeron's share of looted Spanish ships.

At the moment, he was well aware that he had nothing to offer such a woman as a husband. His estate in Galway was run down and needed repairs. To put it in order, he would need gold. And to get that gold, fate was thrusting the buccaneer life on him. It was a situation that one less interested than he might have found ironic.

He said nothing to Céleste d'Ogeron of his thoughts as he stood there, but his eyes took in the red and gold refulgence of the Claro de Luna at anchor in the bay below them. In that galleon, he could wreak vengeance on the hidalgos, but he could do more than that. With that ship he could make a fortune. And Martin Chandos was man of the world enough to know that gold sometimes had more eloquent powers of persuasion with a woman than the most handsome face or the most gifted tongue.

He found Redscar Hudson waiting for him at the Mole. With the Dutchman beside him, Martin Chandos lifted out a sack of heavy gold doubloons and emptied it so that the coins clinked and rolled across the crushed coral paving. The coins brought the buccaneers running, and only Martin Chandos' voice kept them from each other's throats in their haste to snatch at the spilled gold.

"There's more of that to any man that can show me a good score with a musket," he told them, for Martin Chandos knew what damage good marksmanship could do in a sea fight. "Ten pieces of eight as first prize, and five pieces to the next twenty! I'll hold the contest on the stretch of sand beyond the careenage, one hour after the bell on Our Lady of Victory's tower strikes noon."

Redscar's bellowing laugh was echoed by the men. "You'll find more nor twenty lads who can put a ball betwixt the eyes of a charging boar at fifty paces, Captain! These men were hunters afore the hidalgos drove 'em out o' Hispaniola. They've lived by the musket, and they know its use!"

How well Redscar Hudson knew his comrades was proved the next day on the careenage sands. Martin Chandos saw such accurate shooting that he doubled the prize money he offered, and ended up by taking thirty-five instead of the score and one he first had reckoned on.

He left his crew to Redscar, with but two demands. "I'll want men that will take orders. No stupid orders and petty tyranny that you find on a king's ship, but orders in sailing, and orders in keeping the ship clean. I'll stand no filth, for filth breeds disease, and disease can cripple the best crew that ever furled a sail. I want gunners! The best men with a linstock and a match you can find!"

Within two days he had a crew on the decks of the Claro de Luna, swabbing the deck planks and polishing the brasswork at wind vanes and binnacle until it shone. The rigging and new sails that he purchased in the shops along the Rue du Quai were stored below, and the damage that the Hussy's cannon had done was repaired by a ship's carpenter Bertrand d'Oregon himself had recommended. When Martin Chandos was through, the Claro de Luna was a glittering black beauty with golden giltwork at beak and sterncastle, her bulwarks gleaming like ebony, her brass cannons like golden toys in their wreathed gun-port lids. Her oak masts were hung with new sails, and fresh cording sang in her rigging where the wind caught it. Her name he changed to the Moonlight.

Three weeks after the Hussy dropped anchor in Cayona Bay, the Moonlight hoisted her courses and ran out into the strait between Tortuga and Hispaniola with the freshening breeze.

From the patio of the Governor's mansion, Céleste d'Ogeron watched him go, and her blue eyes clouded over as her fingers caressed the hand his lips had kissed. The big Irishman had come to see her several times, appearing once for dinner, twice for cake and wine in the lazy heat of late afternoons.

She had been aware that his eyes had rested ardently on her. Womanlike, she hungered after admiration. What troubled her was the obvious amiability with which her father greeted Martin Chandos' visits.

It bothered the Vicomte de Piercy as well. From her elbow, where he watched the Moonlight swing out into the strait, he growled softly, "I'm not sorry to see him go. Good riddance!"

Chapter Five

THE MOONLIGHT ran like a gull before the wind. She beat westward from Tortuga through the Windward Passage, veering south by southwestward past Jamaica and into the blue wastes of the Caribbean, which the Spanish named *Mar del Norte*.

As an example of the luck that was to make the buccaneers believe in the Little People of whom he whispered with tongue in cheek, and that caused the Spanish to name him Martín el Afortunado, Martin Chandos ran down a great galleon on his fourth morning out of Cayona Bay. She was laboring under the handicap of a sprung mainmast, a leaking hull, and a damaged bowsprit, having been caught in the path of a fierce hurricane that had whipped up out of the Atlantic and hammered in titanic fury across the Antilles and northward to the Bahamas.

Martin Chandos came down on his prey on a southerly tack that brought the Moonlight dead astern of the galleon. He could discern her name through the spyglass with which he swept her hull from the quarter-deck: the Cajamarca. His sakers in the forecastle, set and fired by the gunner that Redscar Hudson had selected as best of all the gunners in Cayona, shattered her rudder at the third ball.

Coming up to windward, the Moonlight loosed a broadside high into the masts and rigging. As she came about to do the same with her starboard cannon, the Cajamarca battered both by nature and by man, struck her colors.

A boarding party discovered a small fortune in pearls below decks. She was bringing the year's supplies from the vast pearl hatcheries at Río de la Hacha, and had ventured alone across the *Mar del Norte*.

Relieving the Cajamarca of her jewels, Martin Chandos generously permitted her captain and crew the courtesy of staying aboard their own vessel, instead of putting them in boats and setting on her a prize crew. It was too early in his cruise to take prizes. And besides, Martin Chandos had something else that he considered far more valuable than a Spanish galleon.

In his search of the Cajamarca's cabin, he had come upon a number of books. Encased in one that had been printed and bound in Seville for the reading pleasure of Don Juan Pérez Guzmán, who was then president of the *Audiencia* of Panama, he came upon a sheet of folded parchment. It was signed by that same Don Juan Pérez Guzmán, and was an express command to Don Diego de Fonseca of the Cajamarca to proceed with all haste to Cartagena, there to join the plate fleet forming with an escort of warships that would safely conduct them all to Cadiz.

What was more important to Martin Chandos, Don Juan Pérez Guzmán had gone on further to give Don Diego de Fonseca certain personal information as to the whereabouts of his brother, Don Hernando, captain of His Majesty's galleon Trinidad.

"This Don Hernando de Fonseca is bringing gold from Panama," said Martin Chandos, spreading the parchment before him on the black oak table of his stern cabin. "Gold in two ships, without escort. Sailing south by east to Cartagena, within a day or two."

He was conferring in the gilded poop castle of the Moonlight with Redscar Hudson, his quartermaster; John Norton, the English gunner; Paul Lascalles, his boatswain; and Dirk Veerhow, his sailing master, a dour, balding Dutchman who seemed more like an Amsterdam merchant than a buccaneer.

It was sober John Norton who offered objections. He grumbled, "Two ships, Captain! Like as not, they'll carry twice the lead we do. It'll be a hard fight to get them both. Besides, they're only a few leagues from Cartagena, while we be far out to sea."

Martin Chandos turned to a map that was rolled to stand beside his chair. He lifted and spread it out. "This is a fine chart, done by Willem Janszon Blaeu himself. We're seventy leagues from Panama, but less than thirty from Cartagena. Assuming the plate ships sail tomorrow, we can be at Cartagena before them, and then, by taking a course due west, we'll intercept their passage somewhere off the coast of Castillo del Oro."

Only Redscar Hudson grinned. The prospect of venturing within sail sight of Cartagena, with its gathered plate fleet, was a prospect to give any buccaneer pause. But so great was his belief in this man who had wrought a miracle with the Hussy against the Claro de Luna and the Concepción that he merely bided his time and watched the others.

Veerhow grumbled in his fat jowls, *"Nein, nein!* I am not liking id. Id smacks too much of taking chances."

The fiery Lascalles added, *"Corbleu!* Taking chances? We'll be cutting our own throats if we move within sight of Cartagena! The Admiral will have every galleon and *gardacosta* outfitted for war. He'll sink us before we can sight Tierra Bomba Island."

Martin Chandos sighed. His blue eyes were swimming in amusement as he moved them from glum face to glum face. "And yet . . . this gold that these ships will carry . . . a year's labor in the gold fields by slaves and captives. It must amount to a fortune."

"Amounts to five hundred thousand pieces of eight," offered Redscar, who had fought with Mansvelt at Curaçao.

Veerhow opened blue eyes wide and puffed out his thick cheeks. "Fife hundred t'ousand bieces!" he repeated, and subsided to whistle tunelessly between his thick lips.

The others stared at Martin Chandos. He shrugged and looked at them. "Is a prize like that worth a little risk?" he asked.

He waited for no answer. He moved past them, leaving them to babble among themselves, while he mounted the ladder to the deck. He ordered more sail crowded on, and directed the helmsman to swing the Moonlight on a southerly course.

They rode south, with the wind abeam and beating steadily across their main deck, for these were the northeast trade winds roaming the Caribbean, and the Moonlight ran with her sails taut before them. At a steady speed, the Moonlight swept down toward Cartagena.

Some twenty miles offshore, Martin Chandos turned the black galleon leeward and let her move down the wind. He posted lookouts in the maintops and spent his waking hours before the gilded taffrail of the poop, with his spyglass trained dead ahead.

"My only worry," he admitted to Redscar Hudson, "is that we'll pass them at night."

And so, when darkness shrouded the Caribbean, the Moonlight hove to and drifted lazily with her mastheads bare, only a spritsail keeping her moving slowly on a gurgling passage. For three days he sailed, and for three nights he drifted, and during all that time he saw no sail or any moving thing other than a score of frigate birds that went swooping past them at sunset of the second day.

It was midmorning of the fourth day, when the sun hung brazenly in an orange sky and the tropical heat bathed men in a thin film of sweat, that the lookout shouted, pointing, "Sail ho! Dead ahead off the larboard bow!" And it was in that moment that Martin Chandos, straightening against the taffrail, caught the golden refulgence of a mighty yellow galleon in the circle of his spyglass. Moving his glass a point to windward, he found her blue consort ship, low in the water, straining every sail to urge her gilded bulk through the azure waters at all possible speed.

The Spanish were wary. That they had seen the black Moonlight as soon as the Moonlight sighted them was evidenced by the speed with which they changed course, veering in a wide circle.

"They'm running back to Puerto Bello," snarled Redscar, peering through the glass. "They'm only a day or two out. They'll figure they can outrun us, or that a *gardacosta* will come along to protect their stern."

"We'll catch them long before either of those events takes place," Martin Chandos told him quietly. "Run up the flag of Spain we found in the captain's cabin on this Claro de Luna. If they're watching us that closely, they may yet figure us for an escort ship come to guide them into Cartagena."

For a moment Redscar gaped, and then he bellowed laughter and went leaping down the poop ladder to the quarter-deck, there to hurry all hands to quarters and direct that the golden lion of Castile be lifted to the main-truck.

For three hours the Moonlight fled westward with the wind aft. In those three hours, the Moonlight gained perceptibly on the yellow and the blue galleons. The weight of gold in the hold of the blue Trinidad held her back, and perhaps half for this reason, half by reason of the flag that floated above the Moonlight's main topsail, the yellow San Antonio hove to and stood broadside on to the approaching Moonlight.

Martin Chandos grunted. "He's a cautious man, that captain. Stand to windward of her!"

It was not his intention to fight the San Antonio, not with the blue bulk of the Trinidad beating leeward with all sails set. He swung by the San Antonio, just out of cannon reach, and bore down on the clumsier Trinidad.

By the time the captain of the San Antonio guessed his purpose, he was a mile astern, and moving away faster than the San Antonio could run. The blue Trindad circled and came about, and the Moonlight was upon her.

Martin Chandos could sail rings around the gold-ballasted galleon, so he tacked in and veered about to rake her rigging with langrel and crossbar. In an hour he had reduced her upper rigging to splintered masts and shredded sails. Her shrouds lay in twisted coils on her deck planks or sinking in the Caribbean, far astern.

He turned his attention then to the yellow San Antonio as it swept up on him.

"Now," he told Redscar, "we'll see how good our musketeers are at picking off living targets."

Redscar sent the buccan hunters aloft, to lock legs in the ratlines or lean from yards and mastheads and send their balls at chosen targets on the San Antonio. Her helmsman went down, as did the man who ran to replace him. Three balls picked off the captain, resplendent in silver-faced breastplate and morion on the quarter-deck. Gunners who sought to reach their deck guns dropped and sprawled.

As his musketeers raked her decks, Martin Chandos smashed the San Antonio with two broadsides. He handled the black Moonlight with an ability he had learned under Christopher Myngs. He hammered her on her starboard side, then turned around and came up on her to larboard. His guns roared until the decks of the yellow San Antonio were a shambles.

The Moonlight slid astern, and her grapnels swung like silver arcs in the sun. They bit deep into wood, and then Redscar brought a boarding party in over the forecastle boards while Martin Chandos swung from the main deck with another crew.

The fight was brief and savage. There were no finer infighters than these buccaneers. Their pistols roared, and their curving cutlasses flashed in the noonday sunlight, until they reddened with Spanish blood. Each man fought his own fight, and the disciplined Spanish soldiers, who were trained not to think but only to obey orders, went down before their surge like tenpins on a bowling green.

Martin Chandos was in the forefront of his raiders. His cutlass was a sweep of steel in his big hand, and the luck of the Galway Irish sat on his shoulders. He drove the soldiery before him, from the starboard rail backward to the poop.

As the Spanish captain cried out for quarter and surrendered his sword, Martin Chandos turned matters over to Redscar Hudson and dove for the companionway. He was learning that the stern cabins of these great galleons contained treasures of their own, in the letters and information they held.

He came to a stop in the cabinway of the sterncastle, with the wooden sills just touching each wide shoulder. His eyes caught and held the woman who stood facing him, her dark, dismayed eyes fastened on his own. She wore a lavender gown fitted with a short bodice and a wide flaring Medici collar of laced taffeta, the corsage of which was so low that the upper swells of her ample bosom were revealed below bare shoulders. Her little hand, which flashed bright with diamond rings under the stern-cabin lanterns, held a long-barreled pistol leveled on him. She braced her wrist on the curve of hip that showed under the loose fall of her skirt.

"Not one step nearer!" she breathed.

He was grimy with gunpowder, and blood was staining his ripped shirt where a sword had streaked across his chest. In his sea boots and black breeks, his wild brown hair tossed loose around his shoulders, he seemed an evil ogre to this Spanish noblewoman.

"Fash, now!" he said easily. "Put up your toy before it goes off and causes harm you can't undo."

Her wide mouth curled, and despite the irony Martin Chandos read on it, its redness and slight moistness gave him pleasant thoughts. She whispered, "What harm could I do, other than kill you?"

He laughed and waved a hand. "Kill their captain, and what would those lads of mine be after doing to you? You'll have heard of L'Ollonois's little cruelties, I'm assuming?"

That Doña Ysabella de Sorolla had heard of Jean David Nau of Ollonne was evident from the abrupt widening of her hazel eyes. Despite the fact that her wrist was jammed against her hips, the long barrel of her pistol wavered.

Martin Chandos held out his hand and came slowly forward.

"Sure, and let's have no more trouble. Give over your toy, and it's myself will see that no harm comes to a hair on your lovely head."

There is nothing so winning as an Irishman with a gifted tongue and a smile to match its eloquence. In a moment the iron barrel of the pistol was in Martin Chandos' fingers, and he was smiling down from his height at her, reassuring her disquietude with his eyes.

Doña Ysabella murmured, "You are not what I pictured you would be, despite the blood and grime on you." Almost unconsciously she put a ringed hand to the russet tresses that she had adorned with a circlet of rose pearls, aware that he was regarding the shoulders exposed by her modish gown with warm eyes.

He laughed shortly. "Oh, it's a pirate I am, in all truth. But not such a one as L'Ollonois and Montbars. It's only gold I want, not torture."

He swung about to the oak chest against the larboard bulkhead. It was richly decorated with marquetry work in the form of fabulous griffons. He opened a drawer or two, and moved on to the wide desk against which Doña Ysabella had planted herself to confront him as he stood in the cabin door. He rummaged in its drawers, lifting out maps and documents, spreading them and reading. One or two of the papers he thrust into his belt.

As the Spanish noblewoman watched him from under half-closed lashes, he moved here and there, examining a few of the books in the rack built into the crimson starboard bulkhead. One or two of these books he placed on the desktop, before he showed his awareness of her scrutiny.

"I'll give you your choice, I will. Stay aboard the Trinidad with the prize crew I set on her, or come aboard my Moonlight. I'll not be able to guarantee your safety here, however."

Doña Ysabella found laughter within her. "Can you guarantee that safety in your own cabin?"

He sighed. "From torture, yes."

Her face was softly triangular under the curling froth of her brown hair. Her forehead was broad and high, and the eyes that mocked him were set apart under thin, curving brows. Her red mouth quivered slightly. He grew aware that her beauty was a challenge.

Doña Ysabella de Sorolla moved toward him and looked up with bright eyes. "I think I find in you more man than pirate. The man does not frighten me, for I have been married twice, and am twice a widow. I will go with you."

She was standing so close that one of her knees, as she moved it forward, brushed against his leg. Flares lighted his eyes, and when the woman saw this she laughed softly, deep in her throat. She went on. "I think it will be a very interesting experience, this visit with you to your stern cabin. It will be something with which to regale the Queen when I return to the Escorial."

With prize crews aboard the blue Trinidad and the yellow San Antonio, Martin Chandos put the soldiers and sailors of the two galleons into their longboats and gave them provisions and water casks. He told the captain, "Hold your course due west, and unless you're a worse sailor than I think, you'll sight land in two days' time."

With that he forgot them. There were other matters calling his attention. In the sterncastle of the San Antonio he had found a sheaf of state documents designed for the hands of Captain-General Don José Jiménez Orozco from his deputy in Panama. Upon breaking the great red seal, Martin Chandos felt the breath rasp in his throat. These were reports on the activities of Don Carlos Esquivel Alçantara, who had taken himself to sea to serve the cause of Spain by assaulting the ships of any who were not subjects of Aragon and Castile, and by his actions prove to these intruding nations that Spain owned all America. Already he had sunk two French barks between the Windward and the Mona Passages, and three buccaneer ketches, and in that same time he had taken two Englishmen and a Dutchman.

His heart slammed in his chest as he read of the destination planned for the crew of his sunken Forthright. The men were to be sent in chains to the mines in Darien, there to labor for the greater glory of Charles II and the empire of the Hapsburgs. The tools that had been the cargo of the Forthright were being put to use, as were the dyes and cocoa that the Dutchman had carried.

In conclusion, Don Ricardo Arroa assured his superior that the "pyrate Spaniard" under command of His Excellency Don Carlos Esquivel Alcantara would continue to sweep *el Mar del Norte* clean of these troublesome riffraff. There was none abler than Don Carlos Esquivel Alcantara at such a task. His ship was the finest ever built in the yards at Cadiz. It carried sixty guns. There was no ship now on the sea that could stand against it.

"Isn't there, now?" asked Martin Chandos of the gathering dusk in his stern cabin as his fist hit the top of the mahogany table.

He rose to pace the cabin floor, from which restless striding he came at last to stand at the stern windows that slanted outward over the white wake behind the Moonlight. Off the larboard stern, the blue Trinidad came laboring against the gold that made its bilge boards creak. His eyes lifted to the reddening sky. Somewhere out on this vast stretch of tropic waters was the Spaniard who had sunk his ship and stolen his crew and cargo and whipped his back to a bloody ruin. His fist struck a carved oak bulkhead.

"I'll find him! If it takes the life of me, I'll hunt him down!"

The creak of a door's hinge brought him around. Doña Ysabella de Sorolla stood in her cabinway, to starboard of the main door. She gestured with a hand and smiled.

"I came to convey my thanks for your generous treatment. My trunks and chests have been stored aboard. I find the cabin you allotted me to be most comfortable."

He bowed and answered curtly, "It's pleased I am to find you so grateful. You may keep to your cabin and be sure that none will bother you."

Doña Ysabella came into the stern cabin, closing the door behind her. She brought an aura of scent in her hair. Her dark eyes mocked him.

"I find you gloomy, señor. And it's no wonder, with the sun setting, and your lanterns unlit for the night."

She struck flint on steel and lighted a taper of beeswax. She moved gracefully from the table lamp to the beam lanterns. In a moment the deepening gloom was gone.

She was close to him by the stern windows as she blew out the taper's flame.

Martin Chandos considered her. He knew that she had come to this tropic world of the Indies to refurbish her fortunes by a judicious marriage. Her own mouth had told him she was twice a widow, and his eyes, roving the lines of her body, told him she would have no difficulty in the task. There were few women as sensual in this new world as Doña Ysabella, and few as intelligent.

As though she took his thought from the eyes that watched her, she laughed throatily. "I can bring more than a body to my marriage bed, Don Martín. I have some jewels and other baubles. Gifts of my two dead husbands. I turned land into gems before I sailed from Madrid."

"Faith, I wouldn't believe otherwise. It's a powerful weight of cannon you carry, indeed."

"Enough cannon to turn me into a buccaneer such as yourself, *señor capitán*. Only my prey is men."

"Rich men." He smiled.

She was a lone and helpless woman, this Doña Ysabella de Sorolla. Her only protection against the rapacity of men and the theft of the jewels in which her fortunes were invested was the body that this buccaneer captain was admiring. And so she moved directly to the attack. She went to his desk, and her white fingers, heavy with diamond rings, moved the papers spread out on its waxed top with a casual air. "With the gold you carry on the Trinidad, you yourself are as rich a man as I'd want to meet."

Her hazel eyes lifted, studying his chest and shoulders, the broad height of him in the simple white shirt and dark breeches and boots he affected on board ship.

Her words startled him. He asked incredulously, "Now, it isn't marriage with a pirate you're proposing for yourself, is it?"

"Other pirates have returned to Europe with fortunes they made here in the Caribbean. Pierre le Grande, El Draque. Only the fools stay on, to drink and gamble away their loot in some buccaneer tavern."

Martin Chandos found himself torn between amusement and amazement. He came away from the dark windows and sat on the edge of the cabin table. As if humoring her, he said, "You'd have to come back to Galway with me. Live on a farm as did my father's wife, and his father's before her."

"There are others of Spanish blood living in Ireland."

"To be sure. Noble gentlemen shipwrecked from the Armada, who found a life of peace better than a watery grave. But surely it isn't serious you are?"

She moved against the leg with which he braced himself on the cabin rug. Her nearness was a blend of milky flesh and rich perfume, and he found that her dark eyes glowed. "Would I be a wife of whom to be ashamed, Martín?"

"It's wasted you'd be on a hillside farm in Galway. Fash, it's wasting time I am to be listening to you."

Her lips smiled at him, and she swayed slightly against his leg. "Take thought on it, señor capitán. We need not return to Galway. There is this whole new world before us. With the gold in the Trinidad and the jewels I carry, we could go far, you and I. In New England, or New Amsterdam, or even in this colony that my lord Baltimore is founding. No es verdad?"

She left him then, moving in her swishing gown to the door of her cabin. For a moment her fingers hunted at its lock, and she withdrew its key. She threw it at him, so that it landed at his foot. "There is no need of locked doors between us, mi caballero!"

The door closed, and for a long time Martin Chandos sat on the edge of the cabin table, staring at the iron key that winked up at him from the rug.

From windward of the coast of New Spain, the Moonlight beat eastward, with Panama astern and all the surging blue waters of the Mar del Norte dead ahead. Martin Chandos stood the quarter-deck with a glass at his eye during the hot tropic days, with the blue sky turning brassy overhead as the sun baked down. He took only moments from his post to snatch at lamantin and baked yams.

He scanned the horizon eternally for sight of a black hull and a spread of white sail, and a ship the Spanish called Vengador. With the luck that was making him something of a legend between forecastle and poop, he came down on two more Spaniards whose hulls were laden with hides and cocoa worth upwards of fifty thousand louis d'or. Off the Swan Islands he ran down a yel-

low frigate that carried gold plate bound for Puerto
Bello.

With four ships in his wake, he made sail for the Windward Passage, plotting a course to bring him midway
between Jamaica and the long green bulk of Cuba. A be-
musement had fallen upon the half-naked cutthroats on
the main deck. A dozen of them would stand at the larboard rail to scan the following galleons, eyes glazed over
as brains that were unused to work labored to calculate
the wealth that was bound for Cayona Bay.

Redscar Hudson, with a toss of his balding head that
made the silver hoops of his earpieces dance, growled, "I
estimate each man jack's share at sixty thousand pieces.
Plague take me if't can be a brass farthing less!" In awe,
the lads would shake their heads and go to lean across the
rail capping and mumble in their beards.

They were running clear off Cape Santa Cruz when
the lookout in the main-truck shouted, "Sails ho! Two
ahead off the larboard bow!"

The spyglass at his eye told Martin Chandos their identity. He brought the glass down with a smile on his
mouth as he turned to Redscar Hudson. "Faith, and
that's a relief. I was after thinking them Spaniards, for
the bigger one is the Concepción that Lizzie Hollister re-
tained for herself. The other is the Hussy."

Redscar looked dubious. "They might be worse nor
Spanishers, Captain. You'm got Sans Espoir on board o'
one, if I know that satanic Frenchman, and Lizzie herself on the other."

There was amusement in the blue eyes with which
Martin Chandos regarded his quartermaster. "You're not
telling me I'm to be wary of them, are you?"

"Sans Espoir thinks you cheated him out of ninety
thousand pieces. What'll he do when he sees you comin'
back, Cayona bound, with them four beauties in your
wake? Won't take no seaman's eyes to judge them all
heavy laden, and not wi' sea shells."

Martin Chandos showed his teeth.

Redscar went on. "You watch! Won't make no mite of
difference to Sans Espoir you're now a member of the
brotherhood!"

"Oh, won't it, now?" asked Martin Chandos softly.

He was aware that his keel was wormy and encrusted
from three long months at sea. She was not so fast or so

maneuverable as when he had hoisted anchor before La Tour. And those two ships sliding to leeward had altered course and were bearing down on him with grim haste.

Redscar muttered, "We might make a deal with 'em. For a share of the merchandise, they might be willing to see us safely into harbor. Sort of an escort, as it were."

"Be damned to your sniveling deals! I need no escort ships to bring in my prizes!"

He went and stood with the wind on his face. It was rising, and it favored the oncoming ships with its steadiness. Martin Chandos leaned across the rail and shouted to the helmsman, "Larboard your helm!" To the worrying Redscar he said, "We'll tack to windward of them."

"You mean you'll try a run for it?"

"That's what I want Sans Espoir to think."

The Dutch buccaneer studied his captain for a moment with glittering eyes. "You'm got a trick in mind, eh, Martin?"

"Not so much a trick as the knowledge of how a man's mind works. This Frenchman considers himself a sailor. He's also greedy. We'll count that pride and greed our allies."

He dropped Redscar Hudson overside in a little tender, with three men to man the oars with him, and written instructions in his pocket. He watched the tender pull for the blue Trinidad before he turned his attention back to the oncoming ships.

A demicannon spoke from the Concepción's beak. Martin Chandos understood it for an order to stand to, but he roared at the men in the riggings, "Crowd on canvas! Up with the mainsail!"

The Moonlight tacked west by south, and drew the Concepción and the Hussy after her. Meanwhile, the Trinidad and the other galleons that the Moonlight had captured between Panama and the Caymans held their easterly course. Now the Concepción was within saker shot of the Moonlight, moving to cross her bow.

The Hussy was nearer even than the Concepción, and exploded a broadside. But the Moonlight was sliding away, and the iron shot fell wasted into the sea.

Meanwhile the Trinidad and her three sister ships were directly to windward of the Hussy. From his post at the taffrail, Martin Chandos watched the blue galleon

veer to come up on the starboard side of the buccaneer
vessel. Redscar Hudson did not wait until the Hussy had
reloaded her guns before he fired. Half a ton of metal hit
the bark with the explosive fury of a tornado. She shuddered under that weight of metal, and wood shattered and
iron twisted. Across the water, Martin Chandos could
hear the screams of men trapped and dying.

The Concepción—to which his spyglass told him Raoul
Sans Espoir had given the name of Victoire—was now
looming off the Moonlight's larboard quarter, and bearing down with all sails full. Her demicannons began talking as Sans Espoir raged on his poop deck.

"It's somewhat overanxious you are, you French
swine," whispered Martin Chandos in his teeth. "To
your jealous rage, which makes you prey on your own
kind, and to the greed that keeps your cannon away from
the Trinidad and those other ships you hope to make
your own, I'll add impatience. It's a trait I'll show you
spells your downfall."

He gambled with time. He let the Victoire empty her
cannon twice, with only shattered channels and a splintered mizzenmast to show for the effort. He calculated
the time it would take her deck gunners to reload and
prime. As the crew on the Moonlight went about its task
of clearing shattered spars and rigging, Martin Chandos
bawled his order.

"Fire now! Larboard cannon!"

The Moonlight swung to the force of its own broadside
as her twenty larboard guns, to which Martin Chandos
had added the weight of the demountable beak and stern
cannons, rocked the Victoire back into the trough of a
breaking wave. Gaping holes showed in her freeboard
bulwarks and just above her waterline. Two chasers
hurled crossbar and langrel in a bloody swathe across the
main deck of the big galleon.

From the ratlines her musketeers began their fire. At
this distance, these wild-boar hunters could scarcely
miss. They picked off helmsman and gunners, and those
who found no single targets directed their fire into the
massed buccaneers, as they slid by the yawing Victoire.

A cheer lifted from the Moonlight's buccaneers. They
clung to scuppers and shrouds as they shook their fists
and roared mocking laughter at the crew on the old Concepción.

"That'll serve ye, you blasted renegades!"

"We'll teach you not to fire on a ship of the coast brethren!"

"Aye! It's the Captain himself what has made cockle-shells of your boats! Ha! And broken them wi' his metal!"

The Victoire fought back with the fury of a dying rat. Now that Raoul Sans Espoir sensed defeat, he became reckless. He hurled every gun on the refurbished Spanish galleon into combat. He took a stand at a gun-port lid, and his voice cracked in a high scream at every successful shot. He almost wrested victory from the defeat of that first smashing broadside. But Martin Chandos was too old a hand at this game of fire and come about, circle and broadside, stand off and hammer away with Long Toms, to be upset by the last convulsions of an opponent.

The Moonlight took metal, and her deck planks were a tangled ruin. But the men ran at Redscar's bellow, and John Norton was calm as he set his guns, and on the quarter-deck Martin Chandos watched the fight through narrowed eyes.

When the black Moonlight next came about, her starboard guns ripped their balls into the crushed and filling starboard quarters of the Victoire. In a haze of gun smoke she pursued a southern tack that ended off the Frenchman's gilded stern. Once again her cannons belched.

The Victoire was a riddled hulk and going down fast as the Moonlight ran to windward of her. Men were dropping from stays and chainwales, or jumping from wrecked decks. A few had climbed into her tender, and were maneuvering in for the others.

From his poop deck, Martin Chandos turned his attention to the Hussy. But that bark was ten thousand yards away, and moving toward the sinking Victoire. He swung about to order his helmsman to put over and run after the Trinidad and her three sister ships, when the lookout roared again, "Sail ho!"

"Where away?"

"Dead off the starboard quarter."

Martin Chandos lifted his glass. For a long moment he froze there.

"What is it, *mi caballero?*"

He whirled to see Doña Ysabella de Sorolla moving toward him from the companionway. He grinned at her.

"The black pirate I've been hunting for three months, only to find when my ship's half wrecked by a sea battle! That ship is the Vengador, Doña Ysabella, out of Puerto Bello, commanded by Don Carlos Esquivel Alcantara— the man who laughed as one of his bully boys lashed my back to a bloody froth!"

Chapter Six

HE WAS IN NO POSITION TO FIGHT. The rigging nets had caught some of the fallen spars and rope, but a litter of torn canvas lay across the Moonlight, and there were men groaning against wounds on the hatches. His channels, to which the shrouds were normally attached, were splintered shards. Ripped sails and loose ropes flapped and swung in the breeze.

"It's a fine morsel we make for yon blackhearted spalpeen," he told the smiling Doña Ysabella. "My crew is in bad shape and the Moonlight almost as bad." He scowled a moment as he stared across the water at the Trinidad and the ships that trailed her. "The gold she carries is fairy gold. Gold that fades with the dawn. The dawn that ends my dream."

And then the optimism that lived in his blood made Martin Chandos shake himself. "Och, why am I talking like a Doomsday prophet? That by-blow hasn't touched me yet with his metal, and it just might be that he'll do nothing of the kind."

Doña Ysabella de Sorolla looked her interest. He caught her by an arm and drew her to the larboard rail. His arm called her attention to the Trinidad and her companions.

"Tell me, Doña Ysabella, what you see when you look to leeward."

"Why," she said, "four noble ships of Spain."

His laughter was hard as he swung her forward so that her eyes could run the length of the Moonlight.

"And now?"

"A Spanish galleon turned privateer."

"Turned privateer! Aye, you know that, as Tara knew the voice of Cormac! But Don Carlos Esquivel Alcantara doesn't know it, and I hope to make sure he doesn't learn it now!"

She whirled on him, her eyes wide. "What madness are you planning?"

"No madness. He sees two pirate vessels in my wake. He'll see the Spanish ensign from my main-truck when I fly it. I'll dip the colors to him as we swing northward, to an apparent rendezvous at Hispaniola, so I will. I've a feeling your Don Carlos will be more concerned with those pirates than he will with five fine ships of Spain."

She gasped at his audacity. The hope that had sprung up at sight of the oncoming black ship quenched itself in the smile she flung at him with a toss of her chestnut hair. "And you'd go back to a farm in Galway! With your wit, you might carve an empire here."

"What kind of emperor do you suppose I'd be making?"

Her eyes locked with his a long moment, as her warm hand came out to grip his wrist. "A fine one, Martin Chandos, with the proper sort of woman at your side."

His laughter carried her to the companionway, along which he watched her move before he took himself back to the quarter rail, to hurl instructions to his boatswain.

The oncoming black galleon swept across the blue water with the lion of Spain flapping at her main-truck. When she saw a similar flag break from the Moonlight, she veered a point and pointed her beak at the sinking Victoire and the Hussy. The two galleons ran within a thousand yards of each other. On his poop deck, where he stood in glittering helmet and back-and-breast, Martin Chandos looked as proud as any hidalgo.

It may have been the sight of the flag or the sight of Martin Chandos himself that convinced Don Carlos Esquivel Alcantara that he was dealing here with five Spanish ships bound for Port-au-Prince on Hispaniola. From his own poop deck he swung a hand from which the thick Mechlin lace fell back like waves shattering on a rock. A grim smile twisting his lips, Martin Chandos waved back.

In that friendly manner they parted, the Vengador sweeping down on the two pirate ships, the Moonlight steadily overtaking its four heavily laden captives.

Bertrand d'Ogeron lifted his head from the circle of pale lamplight that haloed it as he directed his gaze from the sheets of foolscap in his hands to the man who sat at his ease in an oak panel-back chair. The Governor of Tortuga smiled and, lifting his hands, locked them at their fingers, peering over them with hard, bright eyes.

"You're rich, Martin Chandos," he said softly. "The pearls alone would make you that. But the four galleons, the cargoes of cocoa and sugar, the gold plate in the Trinidad, these will make you a legend."

In his blue greatcoat and beribboned doublet, D'Ogeron rose from his black oak desk and moved across the carpet to the window that overlooked the town below. Torches flared along the yellow sands of the curving beach, and lamplight glowed in the narrow, twisted streets. For a few moments he stared at them.

"They're cracking open hogsheads of rum on the beach, and drinking small beer and punch in the taverns. Drinking your health, Martin Chandos. Not since Myngs landed at Port Royal with his loot from Cùmaná and Coro has such a treasure been dumped on a West Indian Island."

The man in the chair smiled grimly. "Some of Christopher Myngs' luck rubbed off on me. I was on his Marston Moor at the time. Later, I was his sailing master on the Centurion. But forget my past. It's something I forgot when I took service under the black flag. How is Ma'mselle Céleste?"

"Confined to her bed. Ill of a fever."

The Governor's face was suddenly gray. Watching him with discerning vision, Martin Chandos found himself alert. "Ah? I did not know. If there is anything I may do to help? If there is a surgeon I might bring from town?"

"What surgeon? Who among those rumpots is fit to— Ah, but I rant. A servant of the West India Company of France must never be ruled by temper. Let's speak of more pleasant matters. Your treasure, for instance. Your share alone is worth over a million louis d'or. What provision shall I make with it?"

Martin Chandos considered. "You've already given me letters of credit on my capture of the Claro de Luna and the Concepción. Deposit these moneys to my credit also, with your company."

Bertrand d'Ogeron paced the room. "No need to repeat the fact that you are wealthy. In France you could buy a château and live like a lord. Frankly, it is against my duty to advise you of that fact. As governor of Tortuga, I work hand in glove with the buccaneers, taking a percentage of their profits for my company. But it so happens I am also a man, and a loving father to Céleste."

A lamp sputtered on the black walnut table. Faintly, through the jalousies, came the sound of many voices roaring sea chanties from the yellow beach. Somewhere in the house a manservant worked with hammer and nails.

Martin Chandos discovered that his heart was hammering in echo to that other hammer. He touched his lips with a dry tongue. "What have I to do with her?"

The Governor turned to the windows and looked down on the town below, as if its sight could loosen the strings of his tongue. To Martin Chandos, his back seemed to stiffen as pride flowed through his veins.

"How can I say what runs in my mind? You have seen Céleste, seen that glowering fortune hunter, the Vicomte of Piercy, mooning over her. Bah! He seeks to bolster the revenues of his impoverished house by allying himself with mine!"

The Governor swung about. His eyes were hard, cold. "I have forbidden him my home, again and again. Yet always Céleste invites him. It is not to be borne! I say to myself. 'If only there were another with whom she might concern herself. Even marry.' And only a despairing echo comes back. Who?"

Martin Chandos took to striding up and down across the thick carpets that gave the room an ornate elegance. He stopped before the rosewood cabinet, heart hammering in his chest. Was this the answer to the meditations that had made him sleepless of late? He recalled his meeting with Céleste d'Ogeron some months before: her talk of imprisonment and her envy of Lizzie Hollister, who was free to do what she willed. They had jested together over a duel. Now that duel was before him, but it was with words that he would fence with the Governor of Tortuga.

"I'll be honest with you," the Irishman said slowly. "I find your daughter mightily distracting. She is beautiful. Accomplished. A gentlewoman, with all the word implies. I've come to know a deep affection for her."

He drew breath into his lungs, aware that Bertrand d'Ogeron was regarding him expectantly. He plunged on, explaining that he saw in Céleste d'Ogeron a woman made to grace the castle halls of his Galway home. Her breeding, her blonde loveliness were echoes out of his past, for he had known in his youth the courts of Scotland and Italy, the royal gardens at Versailles.

True, he was a buccaneer. There was blood on his hands. With shot and cutlass he had ripped gold and jewels from the Spanish. It was not an occupation of which to be proud.

"But a profitable one, m'sieu," said the Governor, his eyes glinting.

"Will a woman reckon profit in a matter of the heart? I've given thought to the matter. Over and over I've wrestled with myself. Men are what fate and their own selves make them. My destiny has brought me to Tortuga and the Main. I can only lay all that before Ma'mselle Céleste and pray her consideration."

The Governor expanded visibly, his smile turning his face into a red melon. "Dear Martin! Why this talk of consideration by Céleste? I am head of my family. In France, as in all continental families, the father rules the home. I will speak with Céleste."

Martin Chandos interrupted, a hand uplifted. "Fash, now! Don't do anything of the kind. It isn't another man I'd have to plead my cause. I'll do it myself, by your leave."

It did not strike Martin Chandos as unusual that they should discuss marriage between himself and Céleste in the absence of the girl. He knew that marriages among those of breeding were made in drawing rooms and salons, by fathers and by mothers, and that women often met their grooms for the first time only weeks or days before their weddings. Remembering the milky skin and blue eyes of Céleste d'Ogeron, he sighed.

"I'd be less than honest," he went on, "not to admit that marriage with Céleste would be a heaven-sent chance to throw over this privateering venture I find myself embracing. It would be a chance to go home, for as the blessed Patrick knows, France is not so far a sail from Galway Bay."

Bertrand d'Ogeron did not dissemble his satisfaction. He rubbed his hands together and nodded his head. "You've no idea what a worry an unwed daughter can be, Martin. Especially one who will come to a groom as well endowed as my Céleste." The Governor cleared his throat, then continued, "You'll be as rich as she, if not richer. Money means nothing to you. I'm safe on that score, and on the score that it's Céleste you love, for herself alone."

The Irish sentimentality of Martin Chandos was touched. He said, "It's setting myself I'll be to win that love. May I see her now?"

A look of alarm touched the Governor's face. He

raised his hands. "She's indisposed. Sick abed. Let me handle Céleste, Martin. Send her flowers, if you will. When she's on her feet, I'll send for you. Meanwhile, be at your ease. I've arranged a house for you, on the slopes below mine. I believe you'll find it to your liking. Win over your buccaneers for your homeward voyage. You'll want some of them as a crew."

On that note, Martin Chandos took his departure from the Governor's mansion. He did not see the cunning smile that curled the lips of the man who stood in its doorway and watched him walk down the stone path. Bertrand d'Ogeron was congratulating himself that at long last he had a weapon to his hand.

The house that Bertrand d'Ogeron had purchased for Martin Chandos was set behind a group of royal palms, halfway between the town and the brick-walled fort that looked out over Cayona Bay. It was a brick and stucco building, low-roofed, with wide windows and a door that was open to catch the cooling night breezes. From the patio a man could sit and survey the high, black crags that closed their rocky claws around the landlocked harbor.

Martin Chandos turned in the doorway to look at that wild stretch of rock and the yellow, curving sands of the careenage, bright with the red flares of a thousand torches. Down there his men held revel, knocking in the wooden tops of hogsheads to get at the rich Jamaica rum. They seemed like toys, far below, and the sound of their rioting and laughter rose to the heights above like something from a dream. There were women down there, drabs from the taverns and brothels: Frenchwomen who had wived with the buccaneers, big-bosomed Hollanders, wenches from London's slums.

His shoulders shrugged a moment as he considered them. In a little while, if things went well with Martin Chandos, he would be putting all this behind him.

He went in the doorway, and stood stock-still.

The living room was ablaze with candles. A great dining table had been set with chinaware and silver service and two tall silver candelabra. Snowy napery covered the polished mahogany, and two matching wainscot chairs were placed at the table's ends. A court cupboard, ornamented with brass mountings, was pushed against a white wall where a number of tall-backed chairs, with their caned backs and arched stretchers elaborately carved in scrolls, flanked a wall table of polished cherry. It was a room as fine as any in the Govenor's mansion on the hill above it.

He recognized the furniture. It had been looted from the sterncastle of the captured Trinidad, and its ornate scrollwork gave the little room a borrowed elegance.

"*Saludos, señor conquistador,*" whispered a throaty voice.

Doña Ysabella de Sorolla rose from the brocaded chair where she had been seated, and curtsied. She wore a Madrid gown of yellow velvet, with delicate Cordoba lace stretched across the bodice. The lace was black, and beneath it Martin Chandos found his eyes surveying the alabaster whiteness of her flesh, as her deep obeisance exposed it briefly. Her eyes mocked him, and he grew aware that Doña Ysabella might be firing the first shot in her campaign for a new husband.

Her liquid Spanish was a temptation in the soft candlelight. "To the victor belong the spoils, *te felicito,* Martín."

"You do not flatter me, Doña Ysabella," he said wryly.

Her glossy brown hair caught the candle flames as she tossed her head. "You are a man, Martín. Any man who feels the flush of success knows that all things are his. Even women captives."

She stepped across the room to him, and taking the full skirt of her yellow gown in her hands, she pirouetted like a Romany dancer. Heady perfume and the scent of powdered flesh came to him, and the challenging mockery of her hazel eyes was like tinder to a wick.

"I have prepared a repast," she told him, her eyes fixed on his. "All day, since dawn, you have been busy on the beach, unloading your loot. You went to see the Governor without even a thought to me. I intercepted his servant as he came searching for you. When I learned of this house, I bade Redscar Hudson fit it out as becomes a great sea captain's home."

"You make free with my things, and with my men."

Her shoulder rose in a careless shrug. "I am a noblewoman of Spain. I am used to commanding in all things."

Martin Chandos grinned, and the devil came and sat in his dark blue eyes. "It would be pleasant work to teach you to obey."

Her eyelids drooped. Sweetly she whispered, "With you as teacher, there are many things I would learn, Martín."

The odor of baking bread came floating from the kitchen, mixed with the tangy smell of roasting beef and simmering turtle soup. The rich cooking smells brought an ache to Martin Chandos. He realized that he had gone without food since dawn, when he and Redscar Hudson had wolfed down cooked turtle eggs.

Doña Ysabella said, "I am so sorry! Your presence made me forget the feast I was preparing. Be seated, will you, please?"

With a swish of skirts, Doña Ysabella vanished into the kitchen. Martin Chandos seated himself at the table, marveling at the miracle that the Spanish noblewoman had wrought with her looted furniture and borrowed silverware.

In a moment she was back, and with her came a tavern waitress, freshly scrubbed and clad in clean gingham. She bore a large silver tray, and on it two bowls of Sèvres ware, from which steam was rising. Martin Chandos laced the turtle soup with sherry, and fell to it with gusto. Across the table Doña Ysabella ate more gently, for her hazel eyes were occupied with his brown face, so hawklike in its frame of long brown hair, and the frippery of black satin and Irish lace with which he had clad himself to visit D'Ogeron.

There was beef that had been buccaned over a beach fire, and heaps of plantains. Following this, a great platter set with salmagundi, a salad of uncooked herbs and chopped palm hearts spiced with oil and garlic, heavy with chopped meat and eggs, was set in the table's center. With silver spoon and fork, Doña Ysabella filled the platter that had been placed before Martin Chandos.

He smiled at her, at ease suddenly, for the food in him and the heat of the candle flames and the rich Madeira with which Doña Ysabella had filled his crystal goblet, were as warming as the lovely woman who served him.

"You show a most interesting domesticity, Ysabella," he said. "I can well believe you were wedded twice."

"Yet never to such a man as you, Martín."

Doña Ysabella gave herself to the salmagundi, aware that her shoulders were pasture for his feeding eyes. Once she raised her blue-veined lids to seek his, and trembled at what she read in them.

Martin Chandos pushed his salad from him and reached for the crystal decanter that was filled with the ruby fire of Madeira.

"I am curious, Ysabella. You have performed such a miracle on the first floor—what have you done on the second?"

Her glass goblet paused in mid-air. She said slowly, "There are bedrooms up above. Two bedrooms."

Martin Chandos let the wine run down his throat. His hand trembled as he placed his goblet on the tablecloth. He pushed back his chair and rose.

"I'm after thinking it's a poor owner I am, to be unaware of my own house. Will you be honoring me with your presence on a tour of inspection?"

Doña Ysabella rose with a rustle of velvet. The wine heightened the color of her cheeks and gave her dark eyes a febrile glow. As she moved past him he put out an arm to grip her around her slim waist and pull her against him. She was a scented, soft thing. It took all his will power to hold her motionless there, and smile down into her flushed face.

"Fash, it's the tempting darling you are! Were I the buccaneer you think me, you wouldn't be safe in the house. But I'm an Irish gentleman too, though God knows I've forgotten it often enough. But tonight's a night I remember it. You sleep alone, acushla!"

And Martin Chandos carried the squirming Spanish noblewoman up the narrow wooden stairs and deposited her in the larger of the two rooms. As he locked the door on her, he grinned in the darkness of the corridor. Doña Ysabella de Sorolla was cursing fluently in liquid Spanish.

For three days Martin Chandos busied himself on the wide yellow sands of the careenage. Stripped bare but for a twist of cloth at his loins, he labored in a pool of his own sweat, scraping the keel boards of the overturned Moonlight. With wooden sticks he plastered her bottom with sulphur against the worms that sought to eat into the wood, then larded over that with thick globs of tallow. Others labored at the seams, calking them with pitch and horsehair. The harsh sound of metal scraping away barnacles and incrustations from below the waterline filled the air.

His meals he ate with Redscar Hudson and the crew, making grins come to their tanned faces as he spoke of his amatory adventures with the maids of Galway in his youth, adventures that had brought him to the decks of ships sailing for the New World from Dublin and Plymouth. He used his Irish wit and charm like a ladle, binding his followers to him in friendly camaraderie.

By night, Martin Chandos moved along the rows of taverns that flanked the great main street of the buccaneer town. He drank mugs of rumfustian with bearded men in petticoat breeches and sashes looped around their middles, and sipped small beer with his gunner and sailing master.

He was tired when he moved up the winding little path that led to the low house where he lived with Doña Ysabella; deliberately tired, so that he could give no thought to the soft white flesh or the hot black eyes that stared so steadily at him.

Before he left Cayona, he would order fresh flowers to be taken by an Indian boy to the Governor's mansion on the hill. Daily he made this a ritual, before he went home. As the days passed, he began to wonder if the flowers reached their destination.

One morning, when he walked with Redscar Hudson on the great mole that thrust out into the blue waters of the roadstead, a cry from his companion sent his eyes searching seaward. There in the narrow opening between two towering cliffs of rock he discovered a bobbing jolly boat.

"Plague take me!" shouted the Dutchman. "I've seen that tender often enough. It's off the Hussy!"

Blood drummed in Martin Chandos' veins. He stepped forward two paces, leaning forward over the splash and gurgle of the water on the rocks below him. From this point of vantage, his eyes strained at the five figures in the jolly boat. Was Lizzie Hollister one of those five? Lizzie, with her tanned skin and black hair, her violet eyes that mocked and taunted, yet could turn so soft and loving under his kisses?

He made out the lean figure of Raoul Sans Espoir, his finery in rags, tugging at an oar. Behind him two others swung long sculls. One slight figure, in shirt and breeches, knelt in the bow. A fifth was bent double, clinging to the staff of the helm.

A crowd began to gather behind the Mole. Here and there a voice jeered.

"It's Sans Espoir, come back with his tail atween his legs!"

"The damned black traitor! We'll string 'im to a china-root tree, eh, lads?"

"Aye! Him an' that slattern wench of his!"

"She'll make a fine sight, adancin' in a slipknot!"

A spill of laughter went up from bearded throats. Martin Chandos knew the bite of anger, then shrugged. Lizzie turned against you in the Windward Passage, his common sense told him. She deserved to suffer any fate these hardened buccaneers decreed. And then his Irish sense of fairness asserted itself.

"Give me your boarding pistol, Redscar."

"Eh? My pistol? What do you— Ah?"

The Dutchman grinned his lewd grin. As he lifted out his long-barreled pistol, he chuckled. "She did something to ye in the stern cabin o' her Hussy, didn't she? Sort o' wedged herself under your skin!"

"Hold your filthy tongue, you red ape," growled Martin Chandos, but he laughed.

With the bearded giant at his side, he moved along the Mole toward the beach, where the jolly boat was aiming her keel. His shoulders forced a passage between growling, snarling buccaneers. They were in an ugly mood, for many of them had been aboard the Moonlight or on one of the four captured galleons in the Windward Passage when Sans Espoir had thrust a fight on them. In their articles, treachery was punishable by death, and word of what the Victoire and the Hussy had sought to do had traveled by lip and tongue from the bay to the heights above La Tour.

Fists shook angrily. Bearded lips growled oaths and hot curses. As Martin Chandos thrust his way between their ranks and to the little curve of sand where the water lapped, voices called out to him:

"Pistol 'em, Cap'n!"

"Aye! Treat 'em as they'd 'ave treated you!"

"Save 'em for hanging! That's what the articles prescribe!"

Twenty feet away, Raoul Sans Espoir leaned on his oar and stared at them. His cheeks were gaunt and unshaven. The skin of his back and chest were burned red

by the sun. His lips were cracked by thirst. His eyes were
mad black dots in his hairy face. Gone was the arrogant
buccaneer captain, and in his place was a man half de-
mented by hunger and thirst.

"Mercy," he croaked. "For the love of God, pity!"

"Come ashore," growled Martin Chandos, waving the
boarding pistol.

A dozen men waded into the clear shallows and hauled
the boat to the beach. Martin Chandos found his eyes
moving past Sans Espoir to Lizzie Hollister. She was in
little better shape than the Frenchman, but there was
pride in her stiff back and in her tilted chin. A white
shirt hung from her shoulders in thin tatters, showing the
dark skin beneath. The remnants of her breeches were
stiff with salt spray, and ripped so that a full brown calf
gleamed in the sunlight.

Sans Espoir tried to stand, but as he came to his feet,
his knee hit the gunwale of the jolly boat and he spilled
forward into the water. Booted feet surged forward, and
in a moment Raoul Sans Espoir became the butt of kicks
and cuffs. Moaning, he clawed his way to the strip of
yellow sand, where he fell and lay gulping in the air.

"Water! For the love of heaven, water!"

Martin Chandos stepped into the water to his knees.
His arms went out and under Lizzie Hollister at knee
and back. He lifted her clear of the thwarts and tramped
upward through the sand with her. Three hard-faced
men moved in a straight line toward him.

The long-barreled gun he held in his hand lifted and
steadied, aimed at a belly. "Move aside, you scum, or I'll
put a lead ball in your guts! I make no war on women."

The steel barrel made a flashing arc in the sun as Martin Chandos brought it across a bearded face, smashing
nose and mouth. He swung it back to strike again, but
the man was on his knees, spitting blood and teeth, and
his two companions lowered their eyes.

"Be glad I didn't use the trigger on him! Now cart him
off, and begone with you!"

Behind him, Martin Chandos heard a man scream in
agony amid a chorus of cursing voices. There was a splash
of water, the high sound of a bone splintering.

Lizzie Hollister whispered brokenly, "I should be back
there with those others. It's only right. By their lights,
I'm guilty of treachery, and deserve to hang."

She was warm against his chest. He remembered those nights on the Hussy, when her gentle fingers had mended his flayed back, and the manner in which she had wooed him back to an interest in life. There was an anger against himself in the bite of his words when he spoke.

"You'll stay where you are, Lizzie darling. I've a house yonder, below the fort. It's there I'm taking you, to be cared for as you cared for me on the Hussy."

And then Martin Chandos thought of Doña Ysabella de Sorolla, and he growled, "There's a Spanish noblewoman there who'll—"

He broke off as she stiffened in his arms. Her eyes glared up from the mahogany oval of her face, dark violet fire under their long, curling lashes.

"A woman? You've made yourself at home on Tortuga, then?"

He flushed. "I sleep alone. I'm holding her for ransom."

Her dark head fell against his chest. It was a perfumed weight, warm and heavy against him. Even half dead from thirst and hunger, Lizzie Hollister was a woman. She murmured, "I must be very heavy. You've been carrying me from the water's edge."

"Fash! It's a mere feather you are. Now be quiet, or I'll be after setting you down on your own two feet to walk the rest of the way."

"I don't have the strength, Martin. And you're so very strong!"

The door to his house was open, for the tropic heat was a living thing that crept everywhere in the island. And then Martin Chandos paused, with Lizzie Hollister there in his arms.

"Faith, it's a suspicious man I am! But I'm not after trusting you to the señora's tender mercies. You'd be safer in the Governor's mansion, until you're on your feet again!"

Chapter Seven

IT WAS TWO NIGHTS LATER that Martin Chandos walked into the candlelit ballroom of the Governor's mansion. The letter with which Céleste d'Ogeron had summoned him found him in a grim mood, for his flowers had elicited no response from the girl he intended to make his wife, and Doña Ysabella was becoming more disturbing, as if sensing the inner hunger that consumed him. The lively kiss Lizzie Hollister had given him, as he set her before the white doors of the mansion two mornings ago, had not helped.

He stood now between a row of bronze candlestands, searching the gathering of buccaneer captains and uniformed French officers of the three ships of the line that swung at anchor below in the bay. Women laughed at their sallies, Parisian tarts sent by the French West India Company to tame the sea rovers to some semblance of order. There were wives and daughters of honest tradesmen, and a few women captives of the privateers who had chosen to live among their conquerors.

As Martin fixed his eyes on the blonde loveliness of Céleste d'Ogeron, his heart thudded wildly. He thought of her father and his words about the young Vicomte, thought of his own run-down estates in Galway that needed the touch of a woman and the sound of a woman to restore them to their old glory.

He hungered to draw her away to some lonely corner and beseech her to look with friendly eyes on him, that he might win her hand in marriage. As if sensing his wish, she turned and stared a moment at him, and there was something of defiance and fright in her blue eyes. Almost imperceptibly she tossed her head, and the Irishman suddenly remembered a colt he had seen broken to the bit and bridle on his father's farm. The colt had been skittish and afraid, yet tremblingly defiant. He wondered why he should think of that colt now.

It was a woman who turned Céleste and pointed out the Irishman to her, and now Céleste came to meet him with outstretched hand. Her blue eyes were feverishly bright, and her cheeks were flushed from the wine.

"It's relieved I am to find you so healthy," he told her

as his lips touched her hand. "I'd begun to imagine you on your deathbed."

"Nothing so drastic. Your flowers hastened my recovery, dear Martin. A dozen every day! An extravagance."

"If they did what you claim, I should have sent ten times a dozen."

Céleste whispered, "I'm going to lose you to Papa. Here he comes now."

Bertrand d'Ogeron made his apologies to Céleste and yoked Martin Chandos by an arm, dragging him out to the jalousied library. He poured Canary from a Laticino glass carafe and frowned slightly. "I've a matter of moment to discuss, Martin. It concerns Sans Espoir and Lizzie Hollister. They blundered against you in the channel south of Cuba. Raoul has admitted frankly that his greed mastered him. Seeing you with those four ships heavily laden, remembering the ninety thousand pieces you took by using his Hussy, he lost his head."

"It's a figure of speech that may prove a prophecy. I understand he's still unhanged; that he talked his way out of a hemp noose down on the sands two mornings ago, as I carried Lizzie here."

The Governor let his worry show in the manner in which he gnawed his lips. "It's about that hanging I want to talk. Raoul Sans Espoir wants to buy his life with gold. He'll give that gold to you and your men, as indemnity. Without intending to sway you, I'll go so far as to say I favor it. Sans Espoir is a good buccaneer when he controls his temper."

Martin Chandos smiled grimly. "By that you want me to understand that he means money to you and your French West India Company. Fash, you have me across a barrel. I can't grant indemnity to Lizzie without extending it to the Frenchman, can I? And I'll never see her swing at the end of a rope. How is she?"

Bertrand d'Ogeron laughed pleasantly. He had his answer, and could afford to indulge his relief. "*Bien! Bien!* Céleste took good care of her. She's back in her own house, well fed and impudent as ever. She's waiting word as to what action you intend to take."

Martin drained the glass, feeling the wine burn in his veins. "I want nothing from her. Nor from Sans Espoir. My men are a different matter. I'll call a meeting and have them assess damages."

The Governor sighed audibly. "I'm relieved. Frankly, I was worried."

"I could have cost you money," Martin Chandos said, and the Governor started and eyed him with new awareness. "But rest easy. Already I think of you as an in-law. I'll take my leave now, to begin my courting of Céleste."

Céleste d'Ogeron was engaged in the minuet, a new dance brought to France less than a score of years before and from there scattered to her colonies. She was graceful and smiling as she made her curtsies and pauses, and Martin saw in her the woman of quality that he had seen so many times in a youth that had known the baronial estates of Galway and Clare. With this woman at his side, he could rule the green fields and farmlands of his inheritance like any country squire.

Something of this mood was in him as he put a hand on her soft arm to take her away from the glooming Vicomte de Piercy, his inner vision blinding him to the young nobleman's scowl. To Céleste he said, "Fash, it's an oven in here. Let's walk a while in the garden."

It was in that same dreaming mood that he led her out through the opened doors and to the flagstoned walks of the little park, aware that she paced meekly beside him, and reading in that meekness an acquiescence to his thoughts.

There was perfume in the garden, and a high silver moon overhead, and a wind whispering among the royal palms. Below them the beach stretched in a white arc beside the dark waters of Cayona Bay, and the lights of the town were pale amber in the night.

"The night has magic in it," said Martin Chandos, with his hand on her fingers as they rested on his forearm. "It's the kind of night when the ghosts of Tara walk again on the Galway hills. You've never been to Galway, acushla, nor seen the farm I own."

He paused as if expecting a reply, but Céleste kept pace with him silently, her head lowered. He went on. "I never thought I'd go back there. It's overrun now, and tenantless. But a man could clear its fields and find new tenants for the houses that dot its hillsides, with the right sort of woman at his side."

They came to a fence of chinaroot that rimmed a drop to the wild jungle below. Martin Chandos turned and caught her hands. There was wildfire running in him that he did not bother to check, fire that blinded him to the fact that Céleste trembled as he touched her.

He cried out, "Marry me, Céleste! Come back to Galway with me! You're the kind of woman fit to queen it at the county fairs, and ride in a fine carriage on the high road. You must know I love you!"

He spoke from the emotions that filled him, and in that same fullness he reached out to catch her in his arms and draw her against him. His strength crushed her. His mouth bent to her lips and held them. He trailed his kisses across her soft cheek and down to her throbbing white throat.

She gasped, "*Non, non!* Please, Martin! Do not, I beg—"

In his hunger and his strength, he did not feel the rigidity of her protesting body. In his zeal, he was deaf to her voice. But when his lips touched her ear, Céleste exploded. She fought him viciously, arms doubled up, thrusting with elbows and palms at his chest, sobbing harshly.

"You dare to kiss me so! Ah, because Papa has spoken to you of marriage with me, you gain courage! You come from Lizzie Hollister to me with your hands all bloody from the men you've killed, so you can pile up gold in France. Ah, go back to her! She is your kind. You'll like her. She'll let you nuzzle her ears. It's an easier way for her to make money than by sinking Spanish ships!"

Martin Chandos stood dumb. There was shock in him, and a dazed bewilderment. This woman with the heaving shoulders and the slim hands working savagely at her torn silk kerchief was not the Céleste he had pictured in his mind, not the loving French girl he visioned in those sleepless nights in the Moonlight's cabin.

"You're no gentleman farmer, Martin Chandos. You're a bloody buccaneer. You're not only a pirate, you're a hypocrite. You steal and murder, and you say to yourself, 'I'm not doing this. I'm really a country squire on a lark.' You look at me and you think, She's a fine lady, the sort of lady that will prove to all the world as my wife that I'm no buccaneer, but a member of the landed gentry. You don't love me. You only justify yourself with me. And—and no word or force from Papa can ever make me change my mind!"

A madness came into Martin Chandos as she ham-

mered at him with her bitter voice. The magic of the
night was gone in the anger that shook him. To hear himself addressed as he was wont so often to address himself,
in the privacy of his own thoughts, added to the rage in
him, until the muscles of his great body quivered spas-
modically.

He did not reply, knowing there was no reply he could
make. He whispered harshly, "By your leave, I'll take
mine!" And then he was brushing past her, striding between the scarlet bougainvillea and the lavender orchids
under the towering royal palms, not seeing the hand she
extended as if to stop him.

There was frenzy in Martin Chandos, and hurt where
her words had scratched his pride raw. He did not reason. He was seeing himself as she had painted him, and
he did not like the sight. Perversely, it aroused something
bestial inside him, that facet of his nature he had
glimpsed when the buccaneers had spread their golden
loot out on the deck of the Hussy.

She called me sea robber! he raged inwardly. She said
my hands were bloody! That I came to her from Lizzie
Hollister! By God! She's no woman at all, but a puling
schoolgirl! Pirate, am I? Buccaneer and sea robber? I'll
be those, then!

The night had lost its magic. Clouds covered the bright
moon, and an eerie radiance cloaked the twisted china-
root vines and streamers of flat-leafed creepers as he
stalked away from the mansion, down toward his house.

Black fury etched his face as he came striding into the
dimly lit dining room, which Ysabella de Sorolla had
fashioned into an ornate replica of the salons she had
known in Madrid. He found a decanter of Madeira, and
drank without bothering to use a goblet. The wine fed
the anger in him.

He took the decanter with him as he mounted the narrow stairs, his blood pounding thickly through his veins.
Buccaneer! Sea robber! Bloody hands! He would teach
her what a buccaneer he was! Aye, and what a lover he
could be to a woman!

A door opened, and Ysabella de Sorolla came out into
the square of yellow light from her room. She stood there
in a thin dressing gown, heavy-lidded, her red mouth
smiling slumbrously.

"Martín? You are well?"

"I'm well," he laughed. "Well enough to go back to sea again."

He walked toward her, not trying to fight the frenzy that shook him. He put up a hand and caught the woman by the long brownish-red hair that trailed down her back. His fingers twisted in that thick hair, urgently.

"I'm a pirate, Ysabella darling! A pirate and a sea robber. My hands are bloody. Aren't you afraid now that they might muss up your hair?"

She laughed softly, wise in her womanhood. "She must have been very bitter with you, Martín, to make you like this."

"I suppose you've a few complaints to make, too?"

Her dark eyes smiled, and her mouth curved softly in the dim light. "I find you more attractive than ever. Anger burns out the gentleman in you."

"I'm not a gentleman any more. Why should I act like one?"

Ysabella did not seem to move, but she stood against him, her flesh soft and warm. She whispered, "Why, indeed?"

He brooded at her, moving his hand against her soft throat. "You're looking for a husband. I went looking for a wife. I hope your luck is better than mine."

The Spanish woman was an opportunist. She lifted her arms until her sleeves slipped back, and then she put them around his neck. "I think I'll test that luck tonight."

"There's no time for that here. I'm putting out to sea before dawn. But it's plenty of time you'll have to find that husband in the cabin of the Moonlight!"

She sighed. "Then I must dress for a sea voyage. It's such a task, when I'm sleepy. Why not come and make that task easier by talking to me, Martín?"

He lifted the decanter in his left hand and drank. When he removed the bottle from his mouth, he said thickly, "I'm in no mood to bandy words."

"Then we need not talk. Just having you there will be pleasure enough."

She went ahead into her room, and Martin Chandos followed her, closing the door behind them.

It lacked an hour to dawn when Martin Chandos went up the rope ladder to the starboard rail of the Moonlight behind the giant Redscar. He had gone himself into the taverns along the Rue du Quai in the cool morning hours, to the barrooms and the little bedrooms above them, rousing drunken men, shaking sober ones. There had been a flame in Martin Chandos that had brought them out of rum-laden stupors or their dreams, without grumbling.

"Up anchor," he told the Dutchman. "I'll be aft in the cabin."

Ysabella de Sorolla stood by the slanted stern windows of the cabin in a dress of white velvet. She looked every inch the *grande dame*, with her fingernails dyed with henna and her sultry eyes blued with indigo in the Moresque fashion.

She went to meet him as he entered, her thick skirts swishing. As he lifted his hands to the lace froth at her shoulders, her eyes glowed.

Martin Chandos twisted his fingers in the lace. He said, breathing harshly, "You look too much the gentlewoman, Ysabella. I'm a pirate, remember?"

"Then make me look like a pirate's woman, Martín!"

His hands went sideways and the white velvet ripped.

It was then that the cabin door swung open.

Martin Chandos whirled, his face dark and hard. "Who in the name of—"

Lizzie Hollister stood in the doorway, her red mouth laughing at him, her violet eyes studying the Spanish woman, who was frantically gathering the remnants of her gown about herself.

Chapter Eight

"I SEEM TO BE interrupting something," Lizzie said, and smiled sweetly at Ysabella de Sorolla.

"Lizzie," said Martin Chandos, opening and closing his fingers, "what in the name of all that's holy are you doing aboard ship?"

She shrugged a shoulder under the loose blouse that was tucked into the wide brown leather belt girdling her tight breeks. "I heard you were setting out on another venture. I thought I'd come along. I'll lose everything from my share of the Hussy's booty, buying back my life."

Lizzie Hollister put out a hand to a dish of fruit that stood on the cabin table. She selected a mammee apple, and her teeth crunched into it.

Over the apple, she looked at them. "I won't be in your way, Martin. I'll be quiet as a warehouse mouse." She went and sat on the edge of the cabin bunk, chewing industriously.

"*Dios mio!*" spat the Spanish woman. "How long do we put up with her?"

Lizzie raised her violet eyes and looked at Ysabella de Sorolla. What the Spanish woman read in those crackling violet depths made her gasp and turn to Martin Chandos. "She will kill me! I see it in her face. She will put a knife between my ribs!"

Martin Chandos looked from one woman to the other. The fury and the hunger in him was seeping away; and when it was gone, the humor of what he saw came and jiggled his ribs. He began to laugh there in the cabin, with Ysabella staring at him as if he had gone mad and Lizzie chewing away on her mammee apple.

Ysabella threw back her head and her dark eyes glistened. "You make a great joke of this, Martin! A joke I do not like! You laugh at the love I offer you. Very well, I will not trouble you again!"

She swung by him, the breath whistling in her thin, patrician nostrils. As if to show him what he scorned, she was careless with her torn clothing, even as her hot eyes challenged him. Then she was moving through the doorway of the starboard cabin, and the door closed.

Lizzie hurled her apple across the room so that it shattered on a bulkhead. "We're well rid of that husband-hunting baggage!" she spat. She rubbed her palms along her breeks, smiling up at Martin. "Besides, she doesn't know what love is."

Lizzie Hollister came to her feet and stretched, and laughed when she saw his eyes moving over her. She came forward easily. "I know what love is, Martin Chandos. You know that, don't you?"

"Lizzie, I—"

She hooked an arm about his neck and leaned against him. Her mouth was only inches from his own, so that he could smell her scented breath. "You do remember, don't you, Martin?"

"By the flaming wheel of Mogh Ruith!" Martin Chandos roared as he put his big hands on Lizzie, lifting her up off the floor and bending his mouth to hers. The frenzy that Céleste d'Ogeron had lit and Ysabella de Sorolla had fed he would expend with this lovely hoyden!

Her mouth was a moist fruit on which he fed. Céleste had told him to seek these lips, to kiss these tiny ears.

And then the starboard cabin came open with a thud.

Ysabella stood framed in the lamplight, her torn garments pinned, smiling gently. "I forgot my fan, Martin."

Martin Chandos swore softly, as only an Irishman can swear. He let go of Lizzie so suddenly that she staggered.

"You've used me enough for your jealousy!" he said when he could. "Take the cabin, both of you. I'll bunk forward with Redscar."

He went out and slammed the cabin door behind him. Ysabella lifted her feather fan and waved it, looking with bright, hard eyes at Lizzie Hollister. Lizzie made claws of her brown hands, and the Spanish woman retreated hastily to the other cabin.

Alone, Lizzie kicked an inoffensive cushion and muttered hot words under her breath.

The Moonlight beat southward past Cap St. Nicolas and out into the Windward Passage. The sky overhead was a brass glare, and the Caribbean surged blue and restless. The wind that had strengthened during the early-morning hours was now filling the great canvas courses until they snapped the taut cordage of their riggings and made the thick oak yardarms creak.

Martin Chandos stood by the quarter rail, once again in breeches and a white linen shirt. His brown hair was gathered at the nape of his neck, and he looked like the Irish gentleman he had always thought himself, until last night in the Governor's patio with Céleste d'Ogeron.

Redscar came to him as he stood before the whipstaff hutch. "The lads be asking themselves if your luck will be as good three times hand runnin', sir."

"It isn't so much luck as knowing the wind and the tides, you big ape. It's the springtime of the year, and the plate ships will be gathering for the summer trip to Spain, for any sailor will tell you that the Atlantic's most quiet in that time."

Below them a roar of laughter went spilling upward into the main course. Redscar laughed softly. "Lizzie Hollister! She's the one for keeping a crew in good spirits. They'd follow her and you to the ends of the earth."

Martin Chandos grunted sourly as Lizzie came swinging up over the rail, the breeze tight against her blouse, her black hair a froth around her tanned face. Cheerfully she waved a hand at the two men and came to meet them.

"How'd he sleep last night, Redscar? Soft as a babe in his hammock?"

Redscar laughed, and Lizzie went on, lifting herself to sit on the capping of the forerail. "I slept easy in his cabin bed. On a nice mattress. A shame he had to give it up. But the Spanish harlot wouldn't let me make him comfortable."

Her violet eyes were laughing at him. Last night these teasing words would have added to the fury in him, but today, with the sky bright overhead and the Moonlight surging through the foaming blue waters, Martin Chandos could laugh too. He threatened, "I'll come back to my own bed one of these nights. Then we'll see how soft you sleep."

A voice spoke behind them. "She needs her sleep, Martin. Come sleep in my bed. I'll warrant you find it warmer than hers!"

Ysabella de Sorolla strolled forward from the companionway, her torn white gown exchanged for a green velvet dress whose boned bodice was set with tiny white bows.

Lizzie Hollister scowled blackly as she took in her elegance. She sneered, "That looks like tougher stuff than the white velvet you tore last night, Martin. Why not try your muscles on it?"

Redscar's bellowing laughter choked off as Martin Chandos gestured. The red-bearded giant went to Lizzie and hooked an arm around her, lifting her and setting her on his hip. "Captain says to take you below, Lizzie. You've had your share of sunlight for a while."

Lizzie screeched and waved her legs, but Redscar moved like an irresistible juggernaut. Martin Chandos watched him a moment, smiling at Lizzie's loud promises of vengeance. When he swung about, Ysabella de Sorolla was at his elbow, regarding him curiously.

"You are a strange man," she said at last. "You are richer than a grandee of Spain, yet you risk all that, and your life, by setting out to sea again. With your fortune, you could be an officer in a European navy. Even win a title for yourself, with the luck your men speak about. And you give it up for this."

"Let's say instead that it's given me up, Ysabella darling."

He walked with her to the starboard rail and scanned the glare of sky and the blue swelling waves. His hand gestured at the white caps and the fleecy clouds in the distance. "It's a big world, this new America. You'll find no titles here, or navies. It puts all men on an equal footing, to let each seek out the level of his own destiny."

"We wax philosophical," she taunted.

Martin Chandos straightened. Far to leeward, like a faint dot against the immensity of water and sky, a ship bore down on them. He touched the spyglass to his eye and studied her.

She was a huge red galleon with thick giltwork at her massive stern cabins and forward beakhead. Her mizzenmast was gone, and the poop yawned empty between goldencrusted railings. The mainmast held canvas that was stripped and shredded as by a claw, the remnants of once proud sails still dangling from the broken mast. There was no fight in her. She yawed and swung to the waves, and her crew was sick with thirst and exhaustion.

A storm had come raging up out of the Antilles to catch her midway between Hispaniola and Cartagena. For a day and a night she had blown straight eastward, before the fury of the storm. She needed food and water badly.

Martin Chandos sent food and water in great tins. In payment, he lightened the hold of the San Pedro of its store of great blue-white diamonds from the washings in Brazil. For two years those diamonds had been stored in the harbor at Havana. Now they were swung in baskets up to the main deck of the Moonlight.

"Only the beginning." Martin Chandos grinned at Redscar, dipping a hand into the maw of a wicker basket. Glittering stones the size of pigeons' eggs trickled through his fingers. "I'll be a pirate and buccaneer as no man ever was before me!"

If Redscar noted the bitterness in his voice, he only shrugged and went on admiring the fabulous gems in the bales dropped here and there on the deck plankings.

That was the start. From off the coast of Cuba, the Moonlight ran south by west, plowing gracefully through the blue Caribbean. She stood off the water routes from Cartagena to Puerto Bello and Vera Cruz like a pacing panther along a game trail.

He was rewarded. Three big galleons came out of the east one afternoon with a mountain of white canvas over their giltwork, three plump birds swooping down on the hungry panther that was the Moonlight.

Redscar took one look at the three ships and shook his red head. "Too many of 'em, Martin. One of 'em be treasure, the other two be fighters."

"They'll all have treasure of one kind or another, Redscar. Crowd on sail. Take the whipstaff hutch yourself."

The red-bearded giant bawled orders, and the crew scurried up ratlines and shrouds like ragged monkeys. These barefooted men clung to ropes with bare feet, and their nimble fingers shook loose sails and courses to the hurrying winds.

The two fighting ships veered to meet the Moonlight. Martin Chandos watched them come, brass spyglass to his eye, a grin twisting his lips. "Here's where I blood my hands a little," he called down to Redscar in the whipstaff hutch. "Hold your course. I'll tell you when to go about."

Lizzie Hollister had come from the stern cabin to stand with Ysabella de Sorolla at the gilt taffrail behind the poop. Ysabella looked the noblewoman she professed to be, but Lizzie was the pirate wench, with two long-barreled pistols in her broad leather belt, her black hair bound in a red ribbon.

Martin Chandos glanced at them and showed his teeth. "If you won't listen to reason and get below, be good enough to stay out of my way."

He took the Moonlight toward the two towering galleons on a straight, mad course that would bring him crashing into their gilded beaks. His men hung over cannon breeches, eyes wide and lips tight and bloodless, eyeing the narrowing gap of blue water between them and those oncoming ships.

And then the galleons slid apart, like the jaws of a hungry animal widening for a meal. They turned south and east, away from their southeastward course. Their maneuver was obvious. They would swing wide of the Moonlight and, between them, batter her to splinters.

Even Redscar added his voice to the chorus of yells that lifted from the gun crews. He growled, "They've caught you this time, Martin! Their ships be jaws to chew us to bits!"

"Have they, now? If you do what I tell you, we'll teach those Spanish dogs what can happen to the jaws of their ships when they try to swallow an Irish pirate!"

The Spanish captains had counted on the Moonlight's maintaining its northwestwardly course. But the Moonlight veered westward when the galleons committed themselves. She came down with all sails humming on tight ropes toward the nearer galleon, the Piélago, offering only her narrow fore view as a target.

The Piélago loosed her larboard guns, but her shot geysered harmlessly into the sea. From the decks of the Moonlight the gun crews could see sudden activity on the galleon, as her captain realized that the Moonlight would soon be dead astern of her, with his own unprotected rudder under her guns. Frantically the galleon attempted to pay off, and in the confusion yawed helpless before the wind.

In that moment, the twenty larboard cannons of the black Moonlight erupted. A rain of iron balls and langrel brought masts down in crashing ruin.

Redscar moved the oak handle of the whipstaff, and the black galleon veered across the wallowing Piélago's sternposts. Hastily reloaded cannon battered her rudder to flying splinters.

Lizzie's laughter rose over the cheering of the gun crews. "He kicks them in the behind, does our Martin! Always!"

The Piélago's sister galleon, the Santa Elena, saw all this, and grew cautious. She came about to maneuver for position. But Martin Chandos had the wind of her, and came up on her stern as a hawk swoops down on a chicken.

He sent Redscar Hudson and a boarding party after his flying grapnels that hooked the blue Santa Elena to the Moonlight. He took a cutlass and thirty howling men, with Lizzie Hollister at his elbow, and followed him.

The trained Spanish soldiery had no time to lock ranks. A dozen half-naked, begrimed buccaneers came flying down from the quarter-deck, led by a cursing, red-bearded giant, and the lines of corseleted musketeers held only until cutlasses flashed overhead. Then they broke and ran, to find Martin Chandos was on them. The fight was brief and bloody between the quarter rail and the foredeck belfry.

When the Santa Elena struck her colors, Martin Chandos placed Redscar Hudson and a prize crew in charge of her cannon, and imprisoned her soldiers and sailors in the hold.

Then the Moonlight and the Santa Elena drove together at the drifting Piélago, whose crewmen were swung overside in a desperate attempt to repair her shattered rudder.

There was no fight. Don Esteban Velasco, who commanded the Piélago, did not deem himself completely a fool. He asked quarter.

The third galleon was hull down on the horizon when Martin Chandos took the Moonlight after her, leaving Lizzie Hollister in command of the surrendered Piélago. The fleeing treasure ship, heavily laden, had no speed to match that of the black Moonlight. Three hours before dusk Martin Chandos came up on her stern and went with John Norton, his gunner, to the chasers on the foredeck. They laid the cannons together and set them high, to topple the lofty masts and their billowing stretch of white canvas.

In an hour the treasure ship was demasted, her decks strewn with shattered wood and ripped sails. Martin Chandos took his boarding crew into that welter of rope and canvas, and inside ten minutes the red bulk of the Felipe Rey was his.

The hold of the Felipe Rey was cluttered with iron-bound chests and coffers, gorged with gold bars and ingots. There were trunks heavy with louis d'or and twin-eagled doubloons. Statues of raw red gold, with rubies inset as eyes and necklaces, stood guard over this fabulous produce of the Indian cities of Castillo del Oro.

Between the rope locker and the water casks, Martin Chandos came on a different sort of treasure. Living treasure. He found red men chained to the bulkheads, sturdy men with hard black eyes and long black hair, proud and sullen in their imprisonment. These were Itza Indians, being shipped overseas to be sold at the auction blocks of Seville.

One of the Itzas knew a few words of Spanish. He was the tallest of the Indians, slim and young and handsome.

"I am cacique," he told Martin Chandos haltingly, as the manacles were being struck from his brown wrists. "Chief, and son of the chief among my people."

He had been captured by armed musketeers guarding the mines at San José. His hate for his captors showed in his glittering eyes, and in the filed teeth he bared as he grimaced.

"I'll set you down on the isthmus," Martin Chandos promised him. "My fight is with the Spanish, not you."

While the treasure was dragged abovedeck and examined by speechless buccaneers, Martin Chandos cemented his friendship with the young cacique, Atalahapa. On a bit of parchment Atalahapa scratched a crude map of the isthmus, with the Gold Road a thin line between Panama and Puerto Bello. To the north he showed where the gold mines were. In those mines, or others near them, the crew of the sunken Forthright worked as slaves.

Martin Chandos put Atalahapa ashore with his companions some miles above Veragua, on the Mosquito Coast. As they parted, the young cacique drew a knife and made a cut on his arm so that the blood flowed. He held his cut to a similar scratch on the Irishman's arm, so that their blood mingled and ran together. He said, "If ever Atalahapa can do a service for Martín el Afortunado, it shall be done. We are blood brothers now."

With prize crews aboard his captured galleons, Martin Chandos steered for Tortuga.

Chapter Nine

THE GARDEN that lay westward of the Governor's mansion was the same as Martin Chandos remembered it, but there was a difference in Céleste d'Ogeron. She was no longer the white-cheeked fury who had sent him raging off to sea some months before. She was flirtatious and apologetic, as repentant as the note by which she had summoned him here to her side on this his first morning on Tortuga.

"You will forgive me my tantrum? I was a very bad girl to be so angry with you. And for such a little thing, like kissing my ear! Here, kiss it for me now!"

She wore a disturbing French scent in the pointed bodice óf her gown, against which his eyes could discern the gentle rounds of her bosom. Her yellow hair tickled his chin as she tilted her head sideways, offering the little pink ear to his mouth.

"Ah? You are bashful?"

She regarded him with slanted eyes: Her mouth pursed itself thoughtfully. "It is perhaps that Doña Ysabella or the pirate girl, Lizzie, have exhausted your desire? *Quel homme!* Not one, but two women he takes with him on a sea voyage!"

Martin Chandos said grimly, "If I did, you drove me to it."

Her glance was arch. "*Ma foi!* You flatter me! Am I the equal of two women in your eyes?"

He had to laugh, and with his laughter, some of the bitterness he had carried from Tortuga to Darien and back seeped out of him. It was with renewed courage that he imprisoned her white hands.

"Then it's letting me hope you are? Giving me to understand that you'll wed with me, and come back to Galway on the Moonlight as my bride?"

She was small in his arms as his big hand turned up her white face to his mouth. He held her to his kiss, feeling her stiffen from her toes to the bright golden flood of her yellow hair. Even through his hunger for her mouth, he recognized her withdrawal. The thought came to him that Lizzie Hollister would not have pulled away like this, or the Spanish woman.

99

He made a loose knot of his arms and brooded at her. "You still don't want my kisses. Fash! I'm no impetuous schoolboy to be forcing them on you. But you're a contrary wench, in faith!"

Céleste d'Ogeron scanned his eyes with her own, seeming to struggle against something inside her that rebelled against this thing she was doing. She whispered, "It's because I can't credit the fact that you love me, Martin. I still feel that you only see in me something out of your past. A symbol of what you hope to be, someday, nothing more."

"What must I do to convince you I love you?"

With a white forefinger she twisted the lace that bedecked his lawn shirt. Her eyes were lowered, veiled by long golden lashes. "I will be honest with you, Martin. I do not love you. I do not think that you love me. But Papa says for me to marry you, and Papa—"

Her breath caught in her throat. Above her lowered head, Martin Chandos scowled out at the blue waters.

He growled, "I'll not be forcing you against your will."

"Ah, now I have hurt you, as I hurt you once before! I am a very bad girl, Martin! I—I might come to love you, in time. If you would be—patient and understanding with me."

She was choking on her words, as if she were swallowing a tidbit that was distasteful, but that for some reason she was forced to eat. "There are many girls who come to love their husbands after they wear a wedding band. I know that, Martin. I—I will be a good wife to you. If you would have me thus, I am willing."

He smiled wryly. "It's no more than I could have hoped for. I've seen you too seldom to have hoped to win your love already. That will be my task after your father has given you to me. I pray you will not regret this, Céleste."

Céleste put her arms around him and, standing on tiptoe, set her lips on his in a cool, chaste kiss. Martin Chandos thought of the fire that lived in Lizzie Hollister, and the different sort of kiss she would have put on his mouth, but he said nothing.

Hand in hand they went to find Bertrand d'Ogeron.

The glass goblet hurtled through the air an inch from Martin Chandos' head and exploded in green fragments against the wall of his dining room. Doña Ysabella was standing on the other side of the table, reaching for something else to fling. Her black eyes were wide, and the shoulders she bared above the lace of her bodice worked convulsively.

"*Embustero! Perro!*" she screeched. "To dare so to treat me!"

"Ysabella! All I said was—"

"I heard you! You're going to marry that whey-cheeked Frenchwoman! Ha! And where does this leave me?"

"Without a husband," he commented dryly.

Doña Ysabella put her hands to the wooden bowl of salmagundi, but Martin Chandos had no disposition to risk a faceful of oil and palm hearts and meat. He caught and dragged her around the table, imprisoning her wrists as she made claws of her hands to reach his face.

"Please!" he growled. "I won't leave you to my buccaneers. I'll set you down somewhere off the coast of Castillo del Oro. You'll be able to reach the mainland from there, and the relatives you tell me live in Puerto Bello."

She panted against him, struggling. "After the months I've worked and tended your home! *Madre de Dios!*"

"You'll be well repaid. A handful or two of choice diamonds. A trunk of doubloons. Ah? That makes a difference?"

Ysabella de Sorolla writhed free, massaging her white wrists where they showed the mark of his fingers. A shoulder lifted petulantly, free of its lace collar.

"A sop to bribe my friendship," she sneered.

"An expensive sop," he reminded her.

Doña Ysabella laughed softly. "You are a big fool, Martín. *Por Dios*, what a fool! Do you think the Frenchwoman loves you? She only sees a good catch in you. It would be better for you to marry Lizzie! At least she'd keep you satisfied. You men! You let pale cheeks and a helpless manner stir your pity, and before you know it, you're in bed with a lump of dough. And all the rest of your life you wonder what happened to the woman you married. She didn't exist, except somewhere in the back of your head, believe me!"

Martin Chandos said stiffly, "I love Mademoiselle d'Ogeron. She is a gentlewoman."

"And her father is a greedyguts who builds his fortune from the blood and gold of Spain!"

Martin Chandos laughed hollowly. "A bystander would think me wedded to you, the way I listen to this tirade."

He stamped from the room, catching up his cloak and beaver hat against the night air. He left behind him a woman furious in injured pride, whose striding took her from the wainscot chairs to the court cupboard, her white hands clutching at the air with long, polished fingernails.

Doña Ysabella conceived herself to be a woman wronged. That Martin Chandos was a buccaneer who preyed on Spain as Spain preyed on France, England, and The Netherlands was forgotten in the tide of her raw anger. At first her proffer of marriage was a gambit to throw him off stride, to protect her from his advances. But the move had backfired, for she had begun to see in him a husband who could bring her a satiation of the senses, as well as a station in life with the gold he piled up in France.

Now that vision was gone. "*Cuerpo de Cristo!*" she swore, and her hand tightened on a candelabra to throw it. "If there were a way of showing him what he has scorned!"

She thought of the bedroom in which he had watched her dress, those months ago, before he had taken her and that pirate wench, Lizzie Hollister, out to sea. He had never come into that room before that night nor after it. Doña Ysabella snarled low in her throat as she mounted the narrow stairs to her bedchamber.

She disrobed in injured pride, posing before the cheval glass in the corner. Over her body she drew a thin robe. Her hair was an unbound russet flood across her gown's collar of Bruges lace. "He shall regret leaving me for that whey-face yet!" she snarled.

"Exactly what I had in mind," said a voice from the open window.

Doña Ysabella whirled. The jalousies at the bedroom window had not been drawn, and through their interstices she could make out a man's lean face and the dangling curls of a glossy black periwig. Then a hand was thrusting the slats up and aside, and Raoul Sans Espoir threw a leg over the sill and moved into the room.

Ysabella de Sorolla regarded him from under frowning brows. "You make free with my bedroom, señor!"

The French buccaneer bowed. "*Pardonnez,* madame! Destiny brings me to you, as it brought you to Martin

Chandos." His narrowed eyes ran over her. He smiled. "I've thought many things of that Irish devil, but never before tonight did I conceive him to be a fool. To possess you, and look elsewhere for his pleasure!"

Raoul Sans Espoir shrugged, and his shrug was an essay on the stupidity of some men. Doña Ysabella read the shrug correctly, and the rage in her yielded to curiosity. Her hand showed him a Farthingdale chair.

"You did not climb into my room to expound on the stupidity of Martin Chandos," she told him.

"*Tiens!* You read me like a book. I'm not here to speak of his stupidity, but of his gold. Of the gold he owns, and of the gold he represents, as long as he's alive to prey on the treasure galleons of Spain."

Ysabella de Sorolla liked the manner in which this courtly Frenchman looked at her. She smiled faintly, and sat on the edge of her bed. "All in all, that is a lot of gold, señor."

"Too much gold for one man. Even if two people were to share it, it is still a vast amount."

Her reddish eyebrows drew together. She said slowly, "Two people to share his gold? In what manner could such an eventuality be brought about, señor?"

He laughed softly, leaning forward. "Spain offers the sum of one hundred thousand pesos for the head of Martin Chandos. Would she not be willing to pay that sum to a noblewoman of Madrid who could send word where Spanish soldiers might trap this Irish buccaneer?"

Doña Ysabella breathed more quickly. Her lips parted and her hazel eyes brightened. "*Sí! Sí!* Spain would pay me well! *Vaya,* how well she would pay! Enough so that I could choose a husband, and not take the first thing in breeches that comes along."

Raoul Sans Espoir chuckled. "You could do that without gold, Doña Ysabella. If I were in the Irishman's shoes—"

Her laughter checked his eagerness. "You would not sleep alone in the next room, *verdad?* But forget me! Tell me of the plan you have in mind."

The Frenchman rose to his feet and strode across the room and back. He said eagerly, "You live with him, even though you claim he sleeps alone. You hear him discuss his sea voyages with that redbeard, Hudson. If I knew in advance where his Moonlight would take him, I could reach Cartagena with the news. You follow? We could trap and cut him to ribbons! Spain would pay you for his head. With all that gold, you would be a rich woman."

Her hazel eyes held steady. "And you?"

He shrugged. "I'd make some claim on his fortune. With him out of the way, I could talk Bertrand d'Ogeron into sharing it with me."

Doña Ysabella frowned. "His marriage may change all this. He won't put to sea again, except to take Céleste d'Ogeron to Europe as his bride. That I should— Wait! He will be off to sea again, for he promised he'd set me down on an island not far from Castillo del Oro!"

The French buccaneer breathed faster. "Ah? So? All that remains is for you to learn the time and place, señora. I will do the rest."

Ysabella de Sorolla allowed herself to be infected with his excitement. Color flamed in her cheeks. "*Sí!* I myself shall spit in his face as they cut his head off! I will teach him what he missed by scorning me!"

In her enthusiasm, Doña Ysabella forgot the thin nightgown that veiled her flesh. It swung open and the Frenchman gasped and whispered, "*Allons!* Shall we seal our bargain in the only way a man and woman should?"

Ysabella de Sorolla found that her frustrations of the past few months were like rich molten metal pouring along her veins. Her blued eyelids lowered and she looked at the Frenchman with hungry appreciation. This one did not lock her in her room lest he be tempted! This one did not put her off with weak excuses! There was no Lizzie Hollister here now, chewing mammee apples!

"*Despacio! Despacio!*" she told him softly as he drew her against him.

Chapter Ten

THE OILY SMELL of rum hung over bare-topped tables
and stout chairs. It filled the tavern that reeked with the
thick smoke of brass lamps and buccaned beef, and the
acrid smell of unwashed bodies. It choked the lungs and
made men cough, but it put fire in their veins. Horny
hands pounded on wood, and a score of voices roared approval of the women who walked between the tables with
trays heavy with sloshing pewter mugs.

"Jamaica rum, bought and paid for!"

"Free, Jeb! Free to drink the Irisher's health!"

"Aye! And good bedding to his bride!"

Laughter rose in the smoke and the thick air. Men in
cotton shirts and plain black woolen breeks sat at the
tables, their arms hooking the waitresses to bring them
down on their laps, to the accompaniment of roaring
laughter.

Only at a table close to the door was there any quiet.
There a gaunt man, whose shirt was a tattered remnant
about thin shoulders, sat stooped over, staring straight
ahead with dull, vacant eyes. His hands were cupped
around a mug that held a tot of gin. Rum was no drink
for Ebenezer Flamm. He wanted the searing flavor of pale
gin in his throat, to wash away his memories.

A woman whose blouse had been ripped from her
plump shoulders careened into the quiet man, giggling
drunkenly. A great bull of a man came after her, reaching out with a hairy hand to finish his destruction of the
bit of linen that still covered her.

The woman slipped and fell into the quiet man, making him drop the drinking can he was lifting to his
mouth.

For the first time the buccaneer who chased the woman
saw the quiet man. He stood swaying, rubbing a hand
across his black beard.

"Eb Flamm!" he gasped. He put both hands to the
table and leaned there, eyes bulging. His voice bellowed,
"As I'm carpenter's helper to Jason Craig! It's Ed Flamm,
boys!"

They came crowding around, for the last they had seen
of Ebenezer Flamm had been when Raoul Sans Espoir's

Victoire had gone down before the roaring guns of the Vengador. Flamm was one of those who had been captured as the corseleted Spanish soldiery had swung from ratlines and shrouds to board the sinking hulk, swords stabbing and musket butts clubbing.

"What'd they do wi' ye, Eb?"

"You look like you been through hell!"

"The mines, Eb? Were it the mines?"

His dead eyes brightened a little as they looked around at the grimy, bearded faces and glittering eyes, the scarred cheeks and sash-draped heads. Ebenezer Flamm felt a little of his old manhood come back into his gaunt body. He filled the beaker with gin and downed it in three swallows.

"The mines, aye. Workin' day an' night wi' a lash on my back. Me and the Dutchmen from the Heyn, and Frenchmen from two cargo ships. Some English lads, too, from the Forthright and the Jolly Bess."

He told them what it was like, the hot days and the sleepless nights, the frenzy for water and good food. The sting and slash of the overseer's whip, the filth and the insects from the marshlands, and the terrible jungle heat that made a man wilt before the day was scarcely begun. The backbreaking labor and the fitful sleep and the food that was not fit for rats.

When he was done, a red-bearded man with a scar across one side of his face stood in front of him, scowling. Ebenezer Flamm did not see him, for his eyes were held by the man at his elbow, a dandy in plum velvet breeches and jacket, his laced shirt fluffed and frilled, a hand on a rapier that swung from a brocaded baldric.

Flamm hiccuped. He said blearily, "Killed a guard and stole a musket an' balls. Got to the coast and stole a pirogue." He shuddered with the memory of those days and nights alone at sea. "It was lucky the ship that found me flew the Jolly Roger and not the lions of Spain. They were homing after two months at sea. They brought me here."

Ebenezer Flamm heard the clink of gold coins. He raised his head and stared at the dandy in the plum jacket and breeches. His eyes fell to the louis d'ors the man held out to him.

Martin Chandos said, "A hundred of these for a quiet talk in my house, after you've celebrated your return. A thousand if you can draw me a map of the isthmus where you worked in the mines."

Ebenezer Flamm laughed until tears runneled his cheeks. "A map of that hellhole? I could draw one with my eyes closed. It'll be the easiest way to make a fortune I know."

Martin Chandos straightened. There was a fever of shame in him, of shame and bitter self-condemnation, that he did not bother to repress. Almost to himself he whispered, "The Forthright! He did say the Forthright, didn't he, Redscar?"

"Wi' my own ears I heard the name, Martin. The men of the Forthright, working in those mines, he said."

Martin Chandos closed his right hand into a fist. He shook it in the air. "Ah, God! That I should have been so blind as to forget the men who came to the Indies with me! They have naught to show for it but whip welts and empty bellies, while I—"

"While you been makin' a fortune and a name that'll bring every man jack here crowdin' to your flag, to sail anywhere you take 'em!"

"I intended taking them back to Europe, those that wanted to come. Now I've a different goal in mind. Puerto Bello! A dozen ships, each armed with fifty cannon. Upwards of fifteen hundred men. They ought to be able to take Puerto Bello, eh?"

Redscar opened his mouth as the conception of what Martin Chandos said hit him. "Puerto Bello, where the Gold Road lies! Her warehouses will be crammed with the yellow stuff about now! And pearls from Isla Rica and diamonds from the Orinoco!"

"And after that, by the grace of Patrick himself, the mines where they dig the gold! To bring those poor devils something more precious than the stuff we take. Freedom!"

The quill pen made a scratching sound as Ebenezer Flamm drew it across a parchment spread out on the great mahogany table. The yellow light of a score of candles illumined the marks and the drawings he had already placed on the wrinkled surface of the vellum.

"Forts and cannon emplacements will blow you out of the water if you move in direct. Better a sidewise attack."

Martin Chandos put a finger into the pool of light that

lay on the map. "That river there. You name it the
Guanches. Could longboats and tenders move up it, to
disembark men? And here—could they move through
forests up behind the city?"

He talked of dismounting cannon and dollying them
through the jungle, of setting them up behind the Spanish guns, to batter them to rubble with the sea walls.

He stood up and moved around the room. Doña Ysabella sat in the shadows, her hazel eyes never leaving him,
her mouth twisted into a cold smile. He took the goblet
of Canary she offered, never glancing at her.

His words were feverish with excitement. "Five hundred men, and only three ships. My own ships! I'll load
them top-heavy with sakers and Long Toms. I'll ballast
them with iron shot and powder. We'll come in at the
Guanches and go overland. We can't fail!"

In the shadows, Ysabella de Sorolla stirred. "You made
me a promise, Martín. You agreed to put me down on an
island from which I could reach Puerto Bello and my
relatives."

"And I'll keep that promise."

Ebenezer Flamm leaned back and studied the map he
had drawn. He said, "There's a score of islands just off
the Mosquito Coast. Any one of them will do."

Doña Ysabella leaned forward so that the candlelight
gleamed on her face, highlighting the brows she arched
so thoughtfully. "But which one? Which one?"

"Here," the gaunt sailor said, stabbing with a finger.
"This one's best for your purpose. Not far offshore, with
a fresh-water lake and fruit trees. *La Isla de los Cuervos,*
the Spanishers call it."

"The Island of the Ravens," said Doña Ysabella, and
smiled to secret thoughts.

Martin Chandos took his leave of Céleste d'Ogeron
with something akin to dissatisfaction in him. He did not
seek to dissemble his annoyance.

"You might show more dismay at my leaving," he muttered. "You'd think you were as eager to see me gone as
Patrick was to see the snakes leave Ireland."

Céleste laughed softly and moved her silk fan back and
forth before the smiling amusement in her blue eyes. She
said, "I am finding in you those gentlemanly instincts
you've told me about. It isn't every man who would turn

from a marriage bed to undertake a rescue of thirty men. Your patience almost matches your nobility of heart."

"You add impertinence to your imperviousness. A quality I might find interesting at another time."

"La, Martin! What need of words like that between us? I'll miss you, truly. But Papa thinks it's such a fine thing you're doing, going to Darien to free your men. I could hardly disagree with him, now could I?"

She was adding to the illusiveness with which Martin Chandos was discovering she abounded. A will-o'-the-wisp was Céleste, a sprite he could not catch and pin down, either to a promise or to a kiss. To himself, Martin Chandos admitted that such illusiveness was a quality to be admired in a woman, but he thought that there were times when a proper amount of surrender would be appreciated.

He made a leg to her as she sat with her skirts spread wide on the marble bench of the mansion patio. He said, "No more than I could depart from you without reminding you of the fact that I love you. I'll be as quick about the business as I can."

Her hand was warm as it caught his arm. "Don't be rash, Martin. The adage that says, 'The more haste, the less speed,' is still a good one."

He thought it odd counsel from a woman engaged to be his wife.

He was returning from the Governor's house along the Rue du Quai when Lizzie Hollister found him. She was coming across the coral street, a gamin in tight black breeks and loose cotton shirt. Two boarding pistols were tucked into her belt, and a great bundle was wrapped and tied on a cutlass scabbard over a shoulder.

He halted, frowning at her. "Now where are those pretty legs carrying you, acushla?"

She tossed her head. "To the cabin of the Moonlight, Captain Martin! You don't think I'm going to let that Spanish cat get her claws into you behind my back, do you?"

"You'll put no foot on the Moonlight this trip, Lizzie! It's no ordinary venture I'm setting out on. I mean to try for Puerto Bello."

She nodded. "Then the rumor's true. Good! It'll make a fine prize."

"Lizzie, I'm forbidding you!"

"Pah! Save your breath. I signed up two mornings ago with Redscar. You'll need a good shot at your elbow."

Martin Chandos considered himself a man of even temper. But this shocking hoyden with the bright violet eyes and all the brown wonder of the skin he could see in the opening of her loose shirt made his patience fall from him.

He caught her arm above the elbow and swung her around, his face hard. "It's the last time I'll tell you, Lizzie darling! You stay on Tortuga."

Her red mouth curved gently. Somehow she contrived to be close against him, and he found her soft and scented and disturbing. "You're so strong, Martin," she whispered. "So strong! Is it thus that you swept Céleste d'Ogeron off her feet?"

He growled and his hand dropped. "A wanton you are, to talk like that!"

Lizzie laughed. "Hire the wanton, Martin! For if I'm a hired hand, I'm loyal to you. If I'm not hired . . ."

His laugh was hollow. "What word of mine could keep you here? Tell me how to forbid you my ship, and I'll do it."

"Then it's settled. I'm a hired hand. In which case, it's only fair to tell you that Raoul Sans Espoir sailed yesterday at dawn."

That touched him. He started back and put his eyes to the blue waters of the roadstead, where a score of ships swung at their anchor chains. His eyes hunted among them, but there was no Victoire II riding gently to the lifting tide.

Lizzie said, "Now, what mission would send Raoul Sans Espoir scurrying off to sea two mornings before you set sail for Puerto Bello? He's been holed up in Cayona for half a year. Now he goes to sea. Doesn't it strike you as odd, Martin?"

He looked down at her and sighed. "He probably wants to recoup the gold his life cost him at the hands of my buccaneers. As you did, on my last voyage."

She shrugged. "You are too trusting, Martin. That is why I come with you—to keep you from making a mistake you'll regret."

And Lizzie Hollister went walking off ahead of him, her round hips faintly swinging, to the jolly boat where Redscar Hudson was waiting.

Chapter Eleven

THE ISLAND was a low length of white coral sand and green jungle. Jagged rocks made a backdrop for the beach that stretched from the blue crystal waters of the lagoon to the first rise of the tangled forest. To the right, a towering cliff fifty feet high, crusted with green creepers, thrust out into the blue Caribbean.

A longboat moved across the blue lagoon, its blades dipping and rising, spraying water. Twenty men sat in the boat, some with chests bare to the tropic sun, some with sashes bound about their heads, some with shaven polls. All of them wore cutlasses in scabbards tied by chains or leather thongs to the belts of their breeks.

Two chests stood on the thwarts, chests of oak bound with iron straps. The woman who sat in the stern rested a hand on the nearer chest, as if to steady it. Ysabella de Sorolla looked sidewise at Martin Chandos where he gripped the tiller beside her. He had been more than generous with the gold doubloons and the diamonds he had pressed on her as a parting gift. He had been so generous that Ysabella found herself close to remorse for what she had done. But the thought of the hundred thousand pesos that Spain promised for a chance to deprive Martin Chandos of his head outweighed that temporary emotion. She set her mouth firmly and stared straight ahead.

The keel of the longboat grated on crushed coral sand. A buccaneer went nimbly overside to his knees in the water, dragging the boat forward. Beyond the black rocks, a score of screeching gulls went flapping upward from the beach.

Martin Chandos gave Ysabella his hand from the boat. As her slippered foot sank into the sand he said, "My men will build you a temporary shelter. We've brought food and a cask of fresh water. The Spanish come here often to hunt, Ebenezer Flamm tells me. You'll be found inside the week."

She walked with him up the slope of beach to the edge of the jungle. The breeze played across her face and ruffled the lace collar at her throat as her eyes roved over the scarlet blossoms and the green vines.

Martin Chandos caught her intent look. "You act as if you expect to find your friends here already."

"No. Oh, no! I was just looking over—"

He was turning away when the flat report of a musket sounded. A feather of his beaver hat went into the breeze as a ball clipped its stem. He swung about and the jungle growths around him came alive with Spanish soldiers in polished corselets and morions. Their faces were savage as they hurtled fallen branches and ran ankle deep in the clogging white sands. A few of them stood, muskets set on crotched barrel rests, firing at the twenty buccaneers who came spilling up the sands to meet them.

"We've come blind to a trap!" Martin Chandos roared, his cutlass whipping out of its scabbard with a scrape of steel.

Ysabella de Sorolla shrank back against the bole of a leaning palm. She ran a tongue over her full mouth, for her throat was dry and hot; and for an instant, as his eyes blazed at her, she thought he was going to slash her flesh with that keen, curved edge.

"It's Sans Espoir laid this ambush for me!" he rasped. "I see him yonder, with the Spanishers. He sailed from Cayona two mornings before me, sails trimmed for a fast run."

And then Martin Chandos was talking no more, but racing across the white coral sands, and his voice was a trumpet that rallied the buccaneers to his side. He came at the Spanish soldiers with his cutlass a whirling circle of steel.

His steel was red in an instant, as he slid under the thrust of a rapier to run his blade through a man's middle. He caught a musketeer and sent him spinning into his fellows. Where the sprawling body made an opening, he dove through.

He fought his way to the Frenchman where he stood a few yards away beside a Spanish officer. Raoul Sans Espoir saw him coming, and hefted the ax he held in his left hand and shook it at him, laughing.

The sight released a black rage in Martin Chandos. His cutlass came down in a wide sweep, and where the cutlass failed its mark, there was his left hand, like a fleshy hook, to lift and hurl men aside.

Men dropped before him and soon only five feet of crushed coral sand stood between Martin and Raoul.

The Frenchman shivered with the hate that filled him. He had a rapier in his right hand and an ax in his left. He said to the Spanish captain, "One side, sir. I alone can handle him. This is what I have dreamed of for almost half a year!"

As he spoke, Sans Espoir hurled himself forward, his rapier a thrust of glittering steel, his ax a wedge of metal to his left. He thrust and he brought his ax around, and Martin Chandos slid low to elude the twin attack.

His cutlass lashed at a leg, but the Frenchman leaped high and his ax came down toward the middle of the Irishman's back. The eight-inch edge bit deep into the sands, for Martin Chandos was rolling sideways and coming to his feet in a fluid motion.

They circled each other, the cutlass a curve of steel slashing in the sunlight, the rapier jabbing and sliding, seeking by its example to lure the cutlass into a thrust so that the ax could come down in a giant circle. They panted harshly, and their boots made shuffling sounds in the hot sands that sprayed as they moved.

"*Corbleu!*" panted Sans Espoir, and came in, slashing down with the ax, holding the rapier poised.

Martin Chandos went back two feet as the Frenchman's forward movement carried him off balance. Then the cutlass was sweeping through the air at the throat of the Frenchman, as he struggled to regain his balance. The uplifted ax handle caught the cutlass edge and turned it.

They circled again, and now it was Martin who thrust in, to be parried.

The shouts of the fighting Spanish and buccaneers sounded louder. Martin Chandos could detect the triumph that made hot music in the brazen throats of his companions. That Sans Espoir heard that betraying note was evidenced from his panted curses.

The Frenchman came in, bending low; and as he bent, his right hand loosed the rapier. His lean brown fingers scrabbled in the sand and came up, and the fingers opened, and the handful of sand he held went showering up and into the face and eyes of Martin Chandos.

"You foul, black-livered spalpeen!" whispered Martin against the pain of blinded eyes.

He reeled back. His boot heels banged hard against an upthrust of jagged coral, and he went down hard on his rump, twisting in his blindness, frantic, desperate.

He heard a screeching grate of steel on rock, and he thrust madly, using the bright steel cup of his bell guard as a mailed fist. He struck with all the fury and the bitterness in him, and the impact of steel on flesh jarred his powerful arm to the shoulder.

He fell in his forward momentum against the Frenchman. He twisted aside in frenzy, before the thought came to him that there had been no life in the man on whom he landed.

Vision came back to his seared eyes in a moment, and he saw Sans Espoir ,twisted there, his head cocked at a grotesque angle on his neck, his eyes white and staring, his thin mouth slack and loose. He lay sprawled over the rock in the attitude his body had taken as that steel bell guard crashed into his neck and broke it. ·

Martin Chandos sighed and got to his feet. His gaze caught the scabbard at his side, its metal jagged and twisted. "His ax hit my scabbard," he muttered. "Sliced off the end. That was the sound I heard when I couldn't see, that sound of metal on rock."

He whirled toward the fighting buccaneers and Spanish soldiery, where they had split into little groups against this game of slash and thrust, hack and parry. He bellowed, and his cutlass waved over his brown poll, and then he bounded toward them.

For an instant the Spaniards held their lines, but the sight of this mad Irishman and the impact of that terrible cutlass he used like a whip were too much for them. They broke ranks and raced across the sands, the howling, gleeful buccaneers storming after them.

And then, from another part of the jungle, a horde of Spanish men at arms came streaming down the sandy slopes. Sunlight caught their bared swords and the long barrels of their fusees. They hit the little band of buccaneers like a tidal wave, sweeping them ahead of them.

Martin Chandos bellowed, but his voice was swept away in the clang of steel blades and the hoarse, sobbing shouts of angry men. These buccaneers who sided him were the finest cut-and-thrust men in the world, but the Spaniards spilling from the tropical jungle were too many to handle.

"To the woods!" he roared. "We'll lose them there."

The move would take them away from the jolly boat and the water lapping the shore five hundred feet southward, but there was no chance to make the boat, not with Spanish musketeers lighting fuses to the touchholes of their muskets, scanning the melee for targets that might separate themselves from the others in the fighting.

Martin Chandos ran in great loping strides, the sand spraying from his boots. The dark green depths of the tropical growth received him like a sheltering cloak. Shot from the Spanish muskets ripped the leaves overhead, spattering him with torn foliage. As he ran, Martin Chandos searched his memory, remembering the island as he had seen it from the jolly boat that had brought Ysabella de Sorolla to the island.

There had been a neck of land thrusting out from the beach some fifty feet high, a growth of coral and sand covered with vines and lignam vitae trees. He hunted for it with his eyes as he ran. His shout carried through the woods, over the thudding pound of the buccaneers' boots: "To me! We'll cut over south, to that spit of land thrusting out into the water."

Someone yelled, "They'll pin us there for certain sure, Cap'n!"

Martin Chandos grinned. "No, they won't! You won't be there when they come!"

The man goggled, but the Irishman growled, "Save your breath for running."

They went through the woods like water through a sieve. Behind them, the Spanish had to go more slowly, for there was always the threat of ambush. Boots left no betraying track on the moist, rotting vegetation of this island floor, as dead leaves and humus sprang back elastically from the feet that pressed them down.

And then the spread of beach was to their right, where the jolly boat bumped its keel on the coral sand four hundred feet away. Ahead of them was the long neck jutting into the ultramarine waters of the Caribbean.

Martin Chandos waved an arm. "To the boat, you men! They want me more than they do you. They might let you make it, if they think they can trap and kill me on the little peninsula."

He gave them no chance to argue, his big hands thrusting them out onto the sand in plain view of any eyes scanning the beach. At their sudden exposure to the brilliant white sunlight, the men roared and began to run like rabbits across the sand.

Martin Chandos watched them go. He tore his scabbard from his belt, that it might not impede his progress as he ran, drawing the soldiery after him. His eye caught the jagged edges of its tip, where Sans Espoir's ax had sheared away the metal. A chuckle shook his body, and then he was moving again, as fast as his boots could find clear going in the tangled growths of roots and creepers.

Captain Luis Valverde stepped from the shelter of an ironwood trunk. On the beach before him sixteen men ran bent over, their sashes flying in the breeze, their shirts ripped and bloody. His patrician face tightened contemptuously.

"Rats!" he told the tropic air. "But Chandos is not among them. He sent them out there to draw my attention, while he escapes another way. But Luis Valverde is no fool, to be tricked by such a ruse!"

His arm swept outward in a curve. His voice hammered at his men. "Spread out! Spread out wide and join hands! You others, form in with pistols ready!"

Hands linked, they made a living chain sweeping that long spit of land like a broom.

When they came out onto the fifty-foot-high cliff that brooded over the water, there was no Martin Chandos to be seen. There was only white coral underfoot, and a few stunted growths, and the wind playing across the waters where a gull dove, and that was all.

Captain Luis Valverde was livid. He scanned the land and searched the blue waters of the sea, and even stared upward where the gull was cawing now, floating on a wind current. He turned his regard to the jolly boat, which was almost out of sight.

He said to the sea and the air, "Somehow he got into the boat!"

A lieutenant at his elbow, a grizzled veteran with gray hair streaking his temples, shook his head dubiously. "I thought of that, sir. I had the boat under my eyes all the time. He was not in the boat. If he had entered it, my musketeers would have cut him down."

A smile came to the face of the Captain. He shrugged and said, "It does not matter. The Admiral is moving in force against his fleet. He got away from us with some devil's trick, but he will not so elude Don José Jiménez Orozco! After all, Lieutenant, even a mad Irishman cannot beat twenty of Castile's galleons with only three."

Chapter Twelve

THE WATER WAS BLUE AND COLD in the springtime of the year. His long dive carried Martin Chandos into those cold depths, down among crusted formations and orange fire sponges, where green sea anemone spread pale tentacles. He swam as he had learned to swim in the water of Lake Ree.

His lungs were bursting, but he did not dare rise to the surface. Somewhere ahead of him was the dark blotch that would announce the keel and curving sides of the jolly boat. But he would never reach it. Not without putting his head above water and betraying his position to the Spanish.

It was not their marksmanship he dreaded, for they were not the equal of his buccaneers with a musket, but the pursuit his discovery would cause. And then, as his lungs grew tortured with the need for air, his hand closed on his scabbard.

He hooked a toe under a coral arch to hold himself underwater; and he put the scabbard into his mouth and cautiously lifted the jagged, twisted tip, sliced by Sans Espoir's flailing ax, into the cool, sweet air. He hung there, swaying to the current, and gulped his fill.

Refreshed, he looked around him. Faintly he could hear the creak of oarlocks, the cadenced chant of the tillerman. Unhooking his toe and thrusting his scabbard in his belt, he swam on.

Just as he was about to turn up for another breath of air, he saw the black shadow of the jolly boat. His hands went out and his feet kicked, and then he was under it, fingers clinging to the keel. As he hung on the boat, he lifted the jagged edge of the scabbard into the air to breathe, while the sixteen oar blades carried him away from the cliff and the Spanish soldiers there.

He came over the main-deck rail of the Moonlight with a dozen hands reaching down to aid him and Redscar Hudson roaring in his ear. Lizzie Hollister was at the giant's elbow, her violet eyes wide and questioning.

"A trap of the Frenchman," he gasped, dripping water as Redscar's hand steadied him. "He learned where we went and brought the Spanishers."

Lizzie said, "That husband-hunting cat had something to do with it, I'll warrant."

He shook his head, chest lifting and falling. "I don't think so. She seemed surprised and frightened. Still, she's found her own kind, and we're well rid of her."

"You get into the stern cabin," Lizzie told him. "I'll bring hot rum and dry clothes. We want you hale and fit for Puerto Bello!"

"Aye! Puerto Bello—and the mines!"

They ran southward from Raven Island, sails bellied full to the steady wind, plowing through the clear waters. The Moonlight showed the way, with the yellow bulk of the Golden Girl, which had been the San Antonio, following astern. The red Heron, once the Felipe Rey, came slicing water abeam.

From the little island to the mainland was only a few miles, but Puerto Bello and her sister city, Nombre de Dios, lay some leagues southward. It was toward these twin cities and the Guanches River, which flanked Puerto Bello to the north, that Martin Chandos laid his course.

It was early afternoon when the lookout in the main-truck sighted three ships to windward, beating up from the Mosquito Coast. Through the circle of his spyglass Martin Chandos could make out the ornate gilded lines of Spanish galleons, sunk low in the water.

"Laden heavy with gold and silver," he told Redscar, handing him the glass. "Heading for Havana with the year's yield from the mines."

Redscar grunted, lifting the long brass telescope. "Do we take 'em, Martin? Or concentrate on Puerto Bello?"

"It's the Gold Road city we're laying our course for."

The redbeard was inclined to argument. "The lads would fight better, knowing there was loot already in their breeches. There's them in the Heron and Golden Girl as never followed you before."

Martin Chandos brooded at his quartermaster. "You're giving me to understand they'd vote to take what's as good as in their hands?"

The Dutchman shrugged his vast shoulders. "I'm telling you straight, Martin. The lads'll feel they don't owe aught to your crew of the Forthright. They go along for the sake of the prize money they win. This is prize money beggin' to be took."

His scowl was dark, but Martin Chandos recognized the honesty of the big Dutchman. He said, "Put it to a vote, then. Signal the Heron and the Golden Girl. I'll speak to them across the water."

The vote was overwhelmingly in favor of attack. Though he was their captain, Martin Chandos knew his was a nominal title, accorded him for the sake of leadership and unity. The vote of the buccaneers was the deciding factor in a crisis. This was the code of the buccaneers, and the Irishman bowed to it gracefully, for he would need their pistols and muskets and cutlasses and their hands at his hundred cannons when he went overland against Puerto Bello.

They stripped the decks for action and laid the cording of the rigging nets. Bare feet slapped deck planks as they ran with shot and powder from the bilge, where they were stored on racks to keep them dry. Redscar Hudson put himself in the whipstaff hutch, for he trusted no other hands than his to follow his captain's orders in a sea fight.

He said as he swung down, "All of 'em be treasure laden, Martin. There's none that are rigged to fight. It'll be easy as robbin' a babe of its sweet-bread stick."

The treasure ships came on steadily, and Martin Chandos leaned frowning on the quarter-deck rail. The mariner in him sensed a trap, but the galleons were so low, so slow under the gold they carried that they could hope to offer little opposition to the trim buccaneer ships that bore down on them.

"Is their captain mad?" he asked Lizzie Hollister. "He comes on as though on parade for the Queen Mother at the sea yards of Seville! He sees us. He must recognize us for buccaneer ships."

"We look like Spanish galleons," Lizzie said.

"Not with our rigging nets swung to catch broken yards and canvas. Not with our cannon showing their mouths like a hound dog his teeth at sight of food. Fash, I'm not liking it!"

He swung the spyglass to his eye again, balancing himself there at the rail. For long moments he studied the oncoming ships, searching their heavy superstructure, the decks aswarm with men. He stiffened abruptly, standing straight and hard.

"They're unloading treasure! Throwing it overside to

lighten themselves! Dumping gold and silver bars into the sea to keep us from getting it!"

Lizzie came to his side, muttering angrily against the trickery of the Spaniards. "Can we come to grips before they sink it all?"

From overhead, where the courses whipped and shook against the wind, the lookout cried harshly, "Sails ho! Twelve to twenty, off to windward!"

Martin Chandos swung about, his glass searching the horizon. He could see them clearly now, fourteen great galleons surging down on him and the three ships he captained. Martin Chandos drew a deep breath.

"It's a trap we've been after running into, as we ran into one on Raven Island, Lizzie darling! A scheming, cunning trap. I've a feeling it's part of Sans Espoir's work."

He brought his telescope back to the three treasure ships now, and bared his teeth in a humorless grin. "It isn't treasure they're dumping, but lead. Lead ingots! Lead as heavy as gold, to sink them low and give them the look of plate ships. Once we committed ourselves—as we've done!—overboard goes the lead and out come the cannons."

Martin Chandos closed the spyglass with a snap of his wrists. "Three against twenty! One hundred cannon against more than a thousand! Bigger odds than the Hussy faced against the Claro de Luna and the Concepción!"

"We can run for it," Lizzie said, breathing faster, a hand curling its fingers over the butt of a pistol at her belt.

The foremost of the three ships sent a ball screaming across the waves. Martin Chandos gestured. "There's your answer. We're almost in cannon range. By the time we came about, those three would be closing with us, long enough to hold us until the others come to grips."

He ran to the rail and shouted down at the buccaneers who were gathered in little knots around their cannons, "Aim high! Fire for their shrouds and courses! Disable 'em! Put as many out of commission as you can!"

He veered, beating to windward. Behind him the Golden Girl and the Heron followed. He swept by the three galleons, a thousand feet abeam of them, and his cannon exploded. Frantically the half-naked buccaneers swabbed smoking barrels. Eagerly their hairy hands lifted and rammed home the powder charges and the round iron shot. Matches flared, were held to touchholes spilling over with black powder.

The Moonlight fired three broadsides at the galleons, broadsides that were echoed by the Golden Girl and the Heron. They came about and ran up the galleons' larboard sides, firing as they went. Every cannon was set high, to hurl its balls at the masts and rigging.

The three Spanish galleons, fighting savagely, were demasted and helpless as the last of the buccaneer vessels showed them her stern.

"They'll not follow us," Martin Chandos said grimly.

"But those others are almost on us!" cried Lizzie.

The Moonlight crowded on sail and fled through the blue water.

The fourteen galleons were not fast. No ship of Spain was a fast ship. But the Moonlight and the Golden Girl and the Heron had been pounded by the three galleons, and word was being howled across the water that the Heron was leaking in her bilge boards.

Martin Chandos sighed. "We'll have to fight."

Lizzie Hollister was sullen. "You're too much the gentleman to be a pirate, Martin. Montbars or L'Ollonois would leave the Heron behind."

He was almost savage as he whirled on her. "Is that the counsel you'd be giving me now?"

She shrugged and turned away, thinking of what the Spanish officers and soldiers would do to her when they took her alive. Her fingers wrapped around the curving pistol butt in despair.

Something of this was in Martin Chandos, for he came striding after her and his big hand hooked under her arm as he swung her around. "They'll never get you to pleasure themselves with, Lizzie darling! I mean to fight, and I mean to go down fighting!"

Lizzie yanked the long boarding pistol from her belt. "Aye, Martin! Those are words I like to hear. They've cornered Martín el Afortunado, but they haven't seen him fight back!"

"A running fight." He grinned, showing his teeth. "With my two best ships against all theirs!"

He swung away, bounding to the main deck. His cutlass slashed the ropes that held the big jolly boat.

"A score of you into this to swing her overside. Then a dozen to take her to the Heron. Bring her crew here and to the Golden Girl. Tell Veerhow on the Heron to stay and turn her into a *brûlot!*"

A howl of glee answered him. Silver hoops danced in ears and mouths widened to shout encouragement. Hands came out to drag the jolly boat to the starboard side and lower her. A dozen men went down on ropes, like supple monkeys.

The fourteen ships of Spain came on proudly. They had Martín el Afortunado where they wanted him. They were closing the nutcracker all around his Moonlight and her sister ships. The Admiral General of New Spain, Don José Jiménez Orozco, stood proudly in his silver-laced armor, a hand on the hilt of the gold-pommeled sword at his side. Ten officers ringed him in on the admiral's walk of his flagship, the Infiernillo.

Don José Jiménez Orozco said, "See how he sends his two-legged rats overside. He thinks to run from us in a jolly boat!" As his officers' laughter rose up around him, Don José added, "The Fortunate One, we call him. It will be the Amputated One by nightfall, when I have him in my hands!" Don José stroked his small black goatee, struggling against the laughter in him. "Behold!" he admonished his officers. "Behold how Martin Chandos would delay us!"

His officers looked obediently where his hand bade them, and saw the Heron with sails trimmed to the wind moving slowly toward the fourteen galleons as the Moonlight and Golden Girl tacked off on a northerly course.

Don José said, "He hopes to sacrifice one ship to gain time to escape! The fool!"

Don José gave orders that were relayed to his fleet. At those orders, six galleons detached themselves to come down on the Heron in a course that would blow her out of the Caribbean under the force of their combined cannons. The remainder of the fleet veered and went after the Moonlight and the Golden Girl.

The Heron held her course, apparently undismayed by the six gilded galleons coming down on her with all sails set. She plowed the blue water steadily, running free.

The watchers on the poop deck of the Infiernillo gaped as they saw the Heron's crew dropping a jolly boat overside. One by one, the men leaped into the water, until the officers around Don José counted twenty. Don José scowled darkly. His mind was going back over talks he had had with Don Miguel Medina, who had captained the Claro de Luna, and with Don Hernando de Fonseca, who commanded the Trinidad and San Antonio.

"Is this some trick of that Irish devil?" he asked his men, and then they all saw the flames licking upward from the hold of the Heron, eating at channels and shrouds and searing the gilded encrustations of prow and beakhead.

"A *brûlot!*" swore Don José. "A fire ship!"

It was more than a fire ship. The six galleons ordered to smash the Heron were within five hundred yards of her when they saw the flames. Under screamed orders, their helmsmen lunged hard on their whipstaffs. Slowly they veered, but by this time the blazing Heron was a hundred yards nearer.

As Don José Jiménez Orozco swore, and as six frantic captains raged on their poop decks, helpless, the Heron exploded.

She came up free of the water, and her sides went out, and there was red flame between the split planks of her bulkheads. Her masts sprang from their stays and the sails went up in writhing tongues of fire. The gunpowder in her hold, stacked barrel on barrel, had been found and devoured by the fire the buccaneers had laid so carefully, before dropping overside to their jolly boat.

There was no escape from the cataclysmic explosion. Bits of flaming wreckage deluged the decks of the six galleons. Their sides sprang and leaked water from the concussion. Men screamed and lay in bloody agony on their decks.

The galleons farthest from the exploding Heron escaped much of the damage that crippled the nearer ships, but their canvas sails were in flames, and desperate crews labored with pails and buckets to douse the woodwork against the blaze.

From the quarter-deck of the Moonlight, Martin Chandos watched the exploding Heron and the resultant terror and confusion on the six galleons. He said dryly, "They'll limp back to port under their own power, but they won't be any good in a sea chase now."

Lizzie choked, "You've lessened the odds by as much as three to one."

"Aye," growled Redscar Hudson from his perch, half in and half out of the whipstaff hutch. "From fourteen to two, it's now four to one. Still big odds, but better than before."

"The odds may lessen even more," said Martin Chandos with a grin. "Observe the Admiral dancing on his poop! He'll have to send healthy galleons to nurse the injured. I've been after giving him a badly needed lesson against the dangers of overconfidence."

Don José Jiménez Orozco did not consider himself a pupil. Any scholarliness that lay in him was blinded by the black rage that swept him. He stamped from rail to rail of the poop, asking the fates what manner of fools were his captains to blunder so blindly into such an obvious trap. Like the supreme egotist he was, he conveniently forgot whose order had sent the six galleons to meet the exploding Heron.

He waved his arms now, shouting like a madman, "After him! I'll flay him alive on my deck! I'll cook him for a week over a slow fire! *Sangre de Cristo!* What things I won't invent to make him scream his lungs out before I deprive him of the tongue with which to do it!"

It was that madness and unreasoning anger on which Martin Chandos counted. As the Moonlight and the Golden Girl fled before the six galleons that came after them, he ordered barrels of gunpowder lowered carefully. On them he set candles in melted wax. "One good strong bump against that barrel," he told his grinning buccaneers, "and the candle will drop into the barrel, and Spain will lose another ship."

It did not work out as well as Martin Chandos planned it. Only one barrel exploded when a galleon hit it. But that barrel blew in the curving sides of the galleon's hull, and inside twenty minutes she was going down by the beak. That loss taught Don José Jiménez Orozco the caution he had refused to learn before.

He put his ships into a fan formation, and with the wind abaft came up on the Moonlight and the Golden Girl, sakers and Long Toms erupting.

The damage that the black Moonlight had taken in the sea fight with the three galleons was telling on her. She fell behind slowly as Don José hurled his flagship and a sister galleon against her. A mast split and toppled down with ripping sails into the nets. A cannon exploded and hurled screaming men and flying metal across the deck.

A breeze that was warm and hot touched Martin Chandos as he stood against the taffrail. From this height he could see the gilded bulk of the Infiernillo as it swept closer and closer, cannons spitting flame. But there was something in the breeze that drew his eyes from the sails of the Spanish galleon to the sky.

To windward, a black cloud covered the horizon, moving swiftly. As he watched it, Martin Chandos felt the change in the air. It grew moist and damp. A jagged line of silver lightning ripped a streak down the scudding greenish-black cloud mass.

"Hurricane!" whispered Lizzie. "Coming fast!"

Martin Chandos laughed bitterly. "The fates are working against me. First the ambuscade on Raven Island, then the trick by which the three galleons engaged me, holding me until those others could catch me. Now this!"

The thunderheads moved swiftly. As the galleons fought across the turbulent blue waters of the Caribbean, the ominously dark clouds rolled overhead, signaling the approaching storm. The wind blew steadily westward from the Leeward Islands, bringing a steady drop in temperature.

That Don José was aware of the oncoming storm was evidenced by the swift recklessness that made him throw every ship he commanded against the Moonlight and the Golden Girl. They came with prows slashing the blue water, every gun mount creaking to the recoil of its belching barrels.

Given another hour, Don José would have smashed Martin Chandos, for the oncoming hurricane gave the Irishman no chance to maneuver and come about. It was a matter of weight of cannon now, and the advantage of that lay with the Spanish. They hammered the Moonlight with solid shot. To leeward, the Golden Girl was beginning to founder.

But the storm hit before Don José could complete his task. First came scudding drifts of rain, lashing men and cannons in sheets of icy water. Surging waves lifted the galleons, swinging them like toys. Sails ripped and blew from their yards as if they were wet parchment. A mizzenmast on the Moonlight snapped as the full force of the wind hit it, carrying it fifty feet overboard.

There was no time to batten hatches or furl courses.

The storm hit with terrifying savagery, in a welter of ripping sails and lifting seas that slapped a wall of water over main deck and forecastle. A dozen men went overside in that first surging sweep of the sea. Blackness closed down on buccaneer and Spanish ships as though the sun had been plucked from the sky, a blackness that was relieved only by jagged stalks of lightning ripping through the clouds.

The Moonlight keeled over, her chains and chain wales under water. The rain became a hail of solid water that ripped men's hands loose from precarious holds on ratlines and shrouds, carrying them overside in the waves that rolled over splintered rails and through the scuppers.

With one hand, Martin Chandos clung to the capping of the taffrail, his voice roaring over the howling wind. "Cut away that debris! Let go the courses!"

There were none to heed him. Men fought for their lives against those towering waves that beat them senseless when they hit. The high, keening wind swept his voice overside with the spilling waters.

Lizzie hung drenched and shuddering against him.

Faintly he heard her voice, though her lips were spread with the shout she was attempting. "It's no use to . . . Can't leave whatever handholds . . . run before . . . hope it breaks before it . . . to the bottom!"

A wave came up like a towering green monster, high over their heads. Martin took one look at it and twisted a big hand in Lizzie's belt. He held her that way, tight to him, as the wave slammed them both against the taffrail.

The wave fell away, leaving them choked and breathless, and then another wave rose to pound them, and after that another. There was no way to measure time in the darkness and the howling wind. Underfoot the Moonlight rocked and shuddered, clawing its way upward from the pounding seas, to shake and quiver as a cross sea caught and wrenched it.

Dimly Martin Chandos was aware that the wind was hurrying the Moonlight before it. In the moments when he could see, with the salt water dripping from his face, his upward glance told him that the three masts had been stripped clean. A few broken ropes waved wildly. As he watched, the foremast gave way and fell with a crack.

The Moonlight leaped and wallowed, surged ahead

before the buffeting wind, and swung as the waves pitched her sideways. Yet always, steadily, she blew westward.

Whether it was day or night when the keel of the Moonlight grated and cracked and fell apart under his boots, Martin Chandos did not know. But the great black galleon halted as her keel was gripped by solid rock and coral reefs, and a billowing wave crested overhead and shook him free of the rail, sweeping him and Lizzie, locked against him, into the cold water.

They plummeted down, blinded and beaten. They came drifting up, turned and tumbled by the surging waves.

And then there was solid footing under his boots, and his legs quivered as he tried to stand, lifting an inert Lizzie Hollister in his arms. A wave smashed him flat, and he crawled on his knees, dragging Lizzie, until the water was gone, and only the blackness and the wind howling overhead remained.

He fell face down beside the girl, and lay unconscious as the hurricane vented its rage over them.

The sun was warm on his back when Martin Chandos woke. His face was half buried in sand that grated his cheek and stung his eyes. But the storm was gone, and the tropic air ran warm and fragrant across the beach.

He attempted to sit up, but he could not move. His arms had been twisted behind his back, and it was as if his ankles were glued together. He rolled over, and between the blue sky and the beach he saw a face.

It was a dark face, streaked with blue paint and blotches of yellow pigment over the cheekbones, and three diagonal green lines at the chin. Tufts of coarse black hair were twisted into a feathered headdress, and he could see filed teeth, long and pointed, between grinning lips.

The Indian held a spear in his right hand. With it he jabbed down at the Irishman.

Martin Chandos discovered he was tied by sisal vines at wrists and ankles. He rolled over, came to his knees, and stood up with a backward twist of his body.

He saw Lizzie then, tied as he was, her white blouse in tatters about her shoulders, only a ragged strip of her breeks remaining. She looked at him with a wry smile.

"This is the same as falling into Don José's hands, Martin. These Indians hate us as much as they do the Spanish, because of the cruelties of L'Ollonois and Montbars."

"What will they do?"

Her brown shoulder moved in the sun as Lizzie shrugged. "They'll chop us into little pieces while we're still alive. Or fill our bellies with wet sand that they'll cram down our throats. Instead of sand, they may use molten gold. Or maybe they'll spread-eagle us over an ant heap and smear us with honey, so the ants will eat us. But whatever way they get rid of us, it won't be an easy death."

Her violet eyes were wide, and there was fear in them. But she smiled as she lifted her chin and looked at him, and Martin Chandos thought, I never knew a braver woman!

Chapter Thirteen

THIS WAS A HUNTING PARTY that had captured them, for they carried no shields, but only long and slender spears fitted with obsidian spearheads. They were tall men, with skin the color of old copper and hair that was black and coarse wound around their heads, falling down in back in a tail. There were ten of them. Feathered headdresses gave them a barbaric look. Their teeth were filed and inlaid with jade.

They marched Martin Chandos and Lizzie back from the beach, into the cool green glades of the tropic jungle. There was rotted vegetation underfoot. The pale boles of ceiba trees, sacred to the Indians, towered high overhead. Twisted vines and knotted tree trunks formed a natural labyrinth through which the natives slipped like shadows. This was the tropical jungle of Darien.

At a bend in the narrow game trail along which they moved, they joined forces with five more natives, who had two prisoners tied at the wrists. Redscar Hudson towered above the Indians, with John Norton at his elbow. The giant Dutchman roared when he saw Martin Chandos. "I was hoping you'd got away from 'em, Martin."

One of the Indians brought the haft of his spear hard against the Dutchman's mouth, and Redscar Hudson rolled on his back in the undergrowth, choking oaths and spitting blood. A hand caught at his torn shirt and pulled him to his feet. He swayed a moment, shaking his head.

There was no more talk. They moved in a brooding silence between the leaning coco palms and rosewood trunks, with dangling bougainvillea vines brushing their shoulders. Pain ran in cramped arms and bunched shoulders and in the wrists where the slender vines were whipped tight.

Once Lizzie staggered and fell against Martin Chandos. Her cheeks were white, but her eyes steadied as Martin Chandos sought them. He whispered encouragement to her, but she only shook her head.

"I might as well die here, Martin, under a spear, as in the fires of their torture," she said brokenly. "I've seen the bodies of white women that fell into their hands.

They pay Spain back, at times, for what Spain has done to them."

She shuddered, and her tongue came out to moisten trembling lips. She went on. "I saw a woman once who had parts of her body burned off. She was still alive, and—"

"By the beard of Niall!" growled Martin Chandos. "That talk only turns your blood to water. Give over, Lizzie."

She said with a sob in her throat, "Be grateful I'm not a screaming maniac, Martin. I know what I'm walking into. You don't."

Dusk was settling over the jungle as they came out onto a wide clearing. A score of rude round huts, whose conical roofs were thatched with palmetto leaves and faced by carved wooden lintels, were set in neat rows about a prayer fire. A hedge of tall poles, their tops carved in human likenesses, stood to one side of the huts.

At sight of the four white captives, children came running, screaming their delight. After them came the women, who snatched up long bare twigs with which to slash the prisoners' legs and faces as they were hurried along.

Here and there, in the huts or scattered near the cooking fires, they could see the wealth that Spanish hands had not stripped from these natives. There were figures cleverly carved from black obsidian, vases and jars of glazed ceramics, necklaces of gold beads and copper bells, and jade and amber combs and ornaments.

The prisoners were marched to wooden cages and roughly thrust inside. Seeing them safely secured, the Indians burst into cries.

"They can't wait for darkness," growled John Norton. "That's when they'll light their fires."

"Fires that will use us for fuel before the sun rises again," said Redscar, nursing split lips with a carefully moving tongue.

A hollow-log drum began to talk, somewhere out among the fires that were being lit against the growing darkness. The sound made a pulsing throb in the night to echo the thudding of the prisoners' hearts.

From the open doorway they could see a stake being lifted and set in a deep hole. Two nearby holes attested the use to which two other stakes, now resting before the fires, were to be put.

The moon was in the sky when they were hurried from the little cages out into the humid night, where the gathered hundreds watched. These were the Itzas, relatives of the Mayas, whom Spanish guns and greed had driven from their strongholds.

Sisal vines were twisted around the men's ankles, which were fastened to cross braces set half a foot above the ground. Their arms were bent behind them and lashed securely to dark hardwood poles.

They brought Lizzie Hollister forward then. Her head was held high.

Martin Chandos said, "Lizzie, I— This is my fault. If I'd only insisted, back there in Cayona, that you stay behind—"

For a moment Lizzie smiled, and her face seemed to glow a little in the light of the fires. "I followed you because I wanted to, Martin. Where you go, I want to go. It's as simple as that. If your destiny ends here, so does mine."

It sounded a little like a marriage oath to Martin Chandos, and he cried out, "Before these devils do something to you so that you can't hear me, I want you to know I—I love you!"

He spoke out of the helpless fury that was in him, in a desperate attempt to salve the pain that would be hers in a little while. It was a futile thing he did, but her response awed him. She looked at him a long moment, and there was pride in her brown face under her loose black hair and in the violet fire of her eyes.

"Ah, Martin! If you mean that, then I don't care what they do to me."

Words came to his lips, there in the firelight, from somewhere deep within him. He said, "It's never a truer word crossed my lips, Lizzie darling!" He thought a moment of Céleste, but Céleste was a soft and pampered woman, and Lizzie Hollister was here, about to die beside him because she had followed him, believing in him as a man, and in his destiny.

Copper-hued hands tugged her back and away from him then, and bowed her back over a flat stone so that she was arched across it. Her tattered shirt and breeks were pulled away and her flesh gleamed in the firelight.

When he realized what they were going to do to her, great beads of sweat stood out on Martin Chandos' forehead. He whispered through trembling lips, "Now may the good God give her of His strength."

They brought glowing coals on flat stone plates, and a priest in a wooden mask came to stand over the prone girl. With metal tongs he lifted a redly glowing coal from a stone plate.

Martin Chandos could not tear his vision from the coal as the priest held it high. He saw Lizzie stiffen while her terrified eyes followed the red cinder approaching her flesh. He saw her eyes close and her small white teeth bite down hard on her lower lip.

Someone cried out harshly from the dark jungle at the edge of the village. The priest straightened abruptly.

A tall young warrior came through the lane opened by his people. He wore a red feather cloak about his shoulders and armbands of solid gold gleamed on his powerful arms. He moved to the stakes that held John Norton and Redscar Hudson. He glanced at the prostrate Lizzie Hollister. Then he brought his dark, glowing eyes to Martin Chandos.

The young cacique cried out sharply. He stepped forward and drew a slim dagger from his girdle of golden plates. Martin Chandos saw him lift the blade and bring it toward him.

"Better to die like this, fast and sure, than—"

The blade did not touch his flesh. It slid deftly between wrist and hardwood stake, and the sisal vines were falling from him. A moment later he stood free.

The young cacique touched Martin on the chest, above the heart. He caught his left wrist and pointed to the thin scar that stood out white against the brown of his skin. The chief said in Spanish, *"Cofrade consanguineo! By this scar in your wrist, we are brothers!"*

Martin Chandos knew him then, and the knowledge weakened his legs. He swayed a moment. "Atalahapa! The Indian I took off the Felipe Rey and set down in Darien! Now, if you aren't as welcome a sight as the face of a lost child to its mother!"

The young cacique called out, and other daggers came to slice the bonds that held Lizzie Hollister and John Norton and big Redscar. They recognized Atalahapa then, and came crowding around, babbling hysterically in this sudden reversal of fortune. Lizzie was taken to a hut and washed and dressed in Indian garments of dyed cotton, open down the sides and belted with a sash of gold plates. Then Indian girls brought bowls of water from a nearby spring, and they drank and sat about a great long table while platters of venison and roasted fowls were set before them. There were tortillas freshly made and steaming, and bowls of vegetable stew.

The young cacique listened attentively as Martin Chandos explained why they had come to this corner of Castillo del Oro. When he heard of the gold mines and the former crew of the sunken Forthright who labored there, he sat a little straighter.

"Those mines are not too far from here. They border the edge of the lands that we Itzas still consider our own."

Martin said, "Can you send men to guide me there?"

Atalahapa showed his astonishment. He wondered if the thought of torture had stolen his blood brother's wits. Did he not know the gold mines were guarded, not only against the escape of slaves, but against the attack of Indians and pirates?

Martin Chandos nodded grimly. "I count on surprise. On surprise, and on the hate with which these slaves regard their Spanish masters. Given a little glimmer of hope, they ought to rebel against the Castile dogs!"

A smile came to the lips of the young cacique as he leaned forward. His great chest lifted and fell, almost as if he labored for the breath that was drained from him by excitement. "There is no way in which to surprise them. You go to get yourself killed or enslaved. The madness of the goddess Ixtab has come to steal your wits. But it is a good kind of madness."

The cacique stood, with the firelight red on his copper skin and on his filed teeth and on the feathers of his cloak. There was exultation in the face he lifted to the sky. "For many years the Spanish have preyed on my people. In the days of long ago, when the caciques ruled at Copán, the people of my tribe were great. Mighty their cities! Strong their armies! Great the magic of their priests! Now those days are no more. The Spanish have brought a blight upon our land."

It came to Martin Chandos as he sat and listened to this impassioned diatribe that this was a voice speaking out of the Mayan past, against the indignities and horrors that had been put upon them by Toledo steel and Madrid gunpowder.

"For once, we of the Itza people would strike back at the oppressors! Not stalking like timid mice among the shadows of the jungle trees, to send an arrow at a soldier, but in full battle array, with our faces and our shields fresh-painted! With our spears and swords blessed by copal incense! We will march with you, my blood brother! Once again the Spanish shall tremble before us!"

It was a wild night, a night of orgy, when these descendants of the rulers of Chichen Itzá and Copán, Yaxchilán and Palenque, feasted on a fermented honey brew mixed with the bark of the *balche* tree. Low wooden tables were brought, so that the four guests could sit cross-legged at them. Roast birds and bread, cacao and cups of honey wine were served.

With Lizzie Hollister close beside him, Martin Chandos ate and drank until the forest and the stars spun around, and a vision came to him of Lizzie cradling him in her arms and weeping gently, and kissing his lips with her red mouth that was flavored with wild honey.

The jungle was a twisted thing, growing in and around and about itself with a mad purposelessness. There were great lignum vitae trees entangled by thousands of tiny wisteria-colored blossoms. There were wide festoons of maidenhair ferns, great trees flowering into puffballs of brilliant yellow, tiny bluebells and riotous red orchids side by side with sister blooms of waxen white.

Deer crossed their path and snakes crawled under their feet. The Itzas, with their broad-bladed machetes, moved at a steady pace. Here the heat was humid and baking, and the chirrup of insects and the occasional roar of a jaguar added to the nightmare illusion through which they marched.

They made progress. By the end of the second day they were moving steadily toward the San Juan River, which they crossed in borrowed *cayucos*.

Sunset of the third day saw them flat on their bellies in matted undergrowth, watching a Spanish sentry in morion and polished breastplate as he walked leisurely back and forth before a great palisade of hardwood logs. They waited there patiently until darkness shrouded the land, and then an Indian at Redscar's elbow came to his feet like a shadow and moved as silently across the grasses behind the sentry.

There were a flash of bronze legs and a movement of bronze arms, and the sentry lay on the ground. Blood dripped from the obsidian dagger in the Itza's hand as he lifted it. The others came forward in a rush of feet, and then the hardwood palisade was behind them and the huts and wooden buildings stretched ahead.

Obsidian spearheads flashed in the light of torches. Voices screamed in Spanish, and throats went raw in curses that suddenly died. There was no confusion on the part of the attackers. Everyone not in chains was an enemy. The Indians slew with a cold rage born of a full century of Spanish rule and torture. \

Martin Chandos snatched a sword from a fallen hand and drove in beside Atalahapa. He could hear Redscar bellow, and the soft curses of John Norton. Lizzie had appropriated two long-barreled pistols, and their thunderous roar sounded now from this quarter, now from that.

To their left were the low wooden huts and buildings where the Spanish soldiers on mine duty were housed. They were ablaze with candles, and in the golden gleam of their flames Martin Chandos could see musketeers running, matchlocks and gun mounts in their hands. They came to a stop on the hard-packed dirt before their shelters, but before they could rest gun barrels on forked notches, an Indian throat sent a howl upward to the starry sky.

There was a whisper in the air that grew louder, a whisper that was echoed by the snapping sounds of released bowstrings. As Martin Chandos watched a Spanish soldier claw blindly at an arrow that transfixed his neck from windpipe to nape, he knew what that whisper was.

"Arrows! Itza arrows!" he rasped harshly to Lizzie, who was drawing a forearm across her powder-grimed forehead.

"Aye, Martin. But not enough of them. Look there!"

More of the hidalgo soldiery were swarming from the long tunnel leading to the mines, swords and pistols naked to the light of the oil torches set on iron stands here and there inside the stockade. A score of Itza warriors went to meet them, but the savages, protected only by round shields of hide and wood, were no match for these seasoned veterans. The pistols flared and Spanish swords stabbed until they were red.

"Lizzie," growled the big Irishman, "if they get the upper hand, we'll wind up in the mines ourselves."

With his captured blade in his hand and with Lizzie at his elbow, he stormed into the Spanish troops. He lunged and parried, thrust deep into a man's throat. A pistol roared in his ears. As a man leveled a musket in his face, a second pistol belched and the man dropped away, a red hole where his face had been under the curving morion.

He covered Lizzie as she dove in to snatch up a pair of fallen fusees from the dead hands. They rocked in her hands as she triggered them at two Spanish swordsmen.

Now Atalahapa was with them, his obsidian dagger glistening red. His savage war cry echoed from the log walls upward past the smoking torches to the open sky. He drove in side by elbow with Martin Chandos, and long rapier and glass knife cleared an open wedge through the Spanish troops, into which came Lizzie and the screeching Itza warriors.

It was the surprise of the attack that had carried them this far, but the surprise was gone now, and officers' voices could be heard lifted in encouragement, shouting orders. Spanish soldiers fell back to regroup.

Now the attacking forces could hear the hum of many voices, the high mad laughter of a screaming man, the rattle of manacles and chains.

"The slaves!" Martin Chandos bellowed hoarsely. "We'll find them eager allies!"

Atalahapa cried out and the Itzas came swarming to him, bowstrings twanging, sending clouds of thin shafts to clear a path. They ran with leaping bounds, glass daggers stabbing, a rapier thrusting, Lizzie's pistols thudding. To one side the burly Redscar Hudson fought with an ax he had chanced on in the forge shed, and with him went John Norton, dagger in his left fist, bare steel in his right.

They hit the troops hastily thrown up in front of them and beat them down with an animal savagery. There was madness in the hearts of the Itzas, for these pale-skinned men in the steel corselets and morions had smashed their people and made them a race of slaves, except for those like themselves who had disappeared into the green jungles. And men like Martin Chandos and Redscar Hudson fought wildly because they knew what a living hell the Spanish mines could be.

Their fury broke the Spanish lines, and the big Irish-man stood with his back to the wooden gate while Red-scar Hudson hacked at the lock with his huge ax. Fists hammered the logs behind the door. Voices pleaded with them, screamed wild curses.

The lock gave with a snap and then the doors were opening inward. Men in rags, with chains around their middles or manacled at wrists and ankles, stood there blinking in the torchlight. Behind them a stench of un-washed flesh and human excrement came out to choke their rescuers.

"By the sacred soil of Aran! It's like a corner of deep-est hell!"

They dove into the filthy hall, a long rectangular building without windows, with soiled grasses spread on bare earth. Men slept here against the walls or in the open center, men who were now standing dazed and incredulous, staring with wide eyes at these buccaneers who burst in on them.

"Praise be!"

"Freedom! Freedom!"

From the body of a dead Spaniard someone dragged a ring of keys. Redscar Hudson came and kept order with his bull bellow, roaring the weeping, hysterical slaves into line, marching them one by one before John Norton, who wielded the key that caused their chains to fall away.

It was Martin Chandos, with Lizzie and her thudding pistols, who took them in a yelling horde across the open space between the slave quarters and the log armory. Some men bent to snatch up fallen pistols and powder bags from dead Spanish fingers. Others grasped dropped swords and daggers, to hurl themselves into the Spanish ranks with a madness born of years of whip lashes and unceasing labor, and food that crawled with vermin.

Martin Chandos got most of them into the armory, where eager, shaking hands clasped at muskets and balls. It was here that Peter Horne, his sailing master off the Forthright, came to pat his back and laugh insanely into his face, whimpering, "Martin! Martin!" over and over again.

He could spare no time for anything but a clasp of hands and an encouraging buffet on the back. Outside, Spanish matchlocks were roaring and men were dying. It was a nightmare scene, with the red torchlight flickering and smoking. Men were screaming in their death throes, but crawling on hands and knees to stab upward with glittering daggers, that others might go on to the freedom they would never know again. Spanish training held the musketeers firm for a little while, but none could stand before these madmen, who welcomed death as a respite from the torture of slavery in a Darien gold mine.

When Martin Chandos and Lizzie Hollister led the main body of the slaves out of the armory, howling and screeching, the hidalgo line fell back. Now these freedmen had weapons to their hands. They set them up, loaded and primed their muskets. They sent a volley into the Spanish line, dropped men here and there.

Redscar Hudson brought twenty men with swords and axes into the Spaniards' flank. They ripped and clawed with bloody steel, folding the musketeers in upon each other. Into that mass of struggling, cursing men the slaves poured their balls.

It became a slaughter after that. The slaves fought with even more savagery than had the Itzas. To them this was a night of which they had dreamed, lying hungry and exhausted or moaning against the whip lashes that streaked their backs and limbs with blood.

The Spanish had no chance to regroup. The better marksmen picked off their officers, and, uncontrolled, they fled into the jungle, streaming out through the open gate to make their way south and west to Panama.

Martin Chandos faced the freedmen in the flare of a score of torches. His chest rose and fell as blood dripped from the sword in his hand. He roared, "I go to Puerto Bello! There are ships in the harbor there. Ships to carry us back to Tortuga. Who among you goes with me?"

There could be no other answer than the bellow with which they lifted up their swords and axes. They shook their weapons in dirty hands, these men who had seen a miracle come to life under their eyes. There were Englishmen and Frenchmen, Dutch and Italians, mixed with Indians. All manner of men were here but Spanish, living proof that Spain held all in the New World to be her enemies.

Martin Chandos found only a dozen of his crew from the Forthright still alive. They crowded around, calling blessings on him, faces wet with tears, caressing the Irishman's arms with fingers that shook. He talked an hour with them, promising them good shares from his buccaneering ventures.

Atalahapa gave Martin Chandos three Itza warriors as his guides. The young cacique said, "They will take you by the swiftest route to the city the Spaniards name Puerto Bello."

"And a ship to take us home, to Tortuga," echoed Redscar Hudson.

Chapter Fourteen

THE MOON was a silver ball overhead as Martin Chandos shifted against the sleeplessness in him. He strove for relaxation on the hard ground and on the folded shirt under his head. A shadow fell across his face and, looking up, he saw Lizzie.

She came down on her knees beside him, sitting back on her calves. Her tattered blouse and jagged breeks were gone, and she was like some barbaric princess in an Itza skirt decorated with the kneeling figure of Itzamna, the sky god. Across her bosom was a twisted length of white cloth.

"We've come a long way together, Martin," she said.

She was no longer the wild buccaneer wench who had doctored him back to life in the cabin of the Hussy. There was a shyness about her, a modesty that revealed itself in the long lashes that veiled her violet eyes from him.

Martin Chandos put a hand on her arm, wondering at its quiver. Something full and heavy surged in him before this kneeling woman. His heart was thudding. He said, "You've been more than a companion, Lizzie. You've been a friend and helpmate."

"Those are good things to be to a man like you, Martin."

He sat up. Now her knees pressed into his thigh, and it may have been that pressure, or the heat of the darkened jungle, that made his breath come faster. He let his eyes move over her brown, smooth shoulders and the tightness of her Itza skirt about her hips. Her legs were slim and strong down to the deerskin sandals that protected her feet.

She was a white Indian, kneeling here, a woodland creature of the jungles, a sprite come in the silver moonlight to his side. A wild urgency to taste the wild honey of her lips flooded him now.

He pulled her against him and she lay captive there, soft and warm. He had no recollection of moving his head, but her lips were on his and they clung like that, tight to each other, shaking a little in the hunger that spilled through them.

"Martin," she breathed. "Oh, Martin!"

Her hand twisted in his long brown hair, holding his head so that she could read his hot blue eyes. What she saw there made her bow her face and press it into his chest.

"You told me once you loved me. Do you remember that? In the Itza village, when they were going to put live coals on me?"

· "I remember," he told her hoarsely.

"Was it just to give me courage, Martin? Was that all you meant when you said that?"

Martin Chandos could not speak against the hunger and the want in him. No woman had ever affected him as this barbaric witch was doing, with her wide eyes and quivering mouth and the thick black hair scented with some Itza perfume. Her courage on the march from the Indian village to the mines, the ferocity with which she had thrown herself at armored soldiers, the eagerness and unflagging spirit with which she walked ankle-deep in rotten vegetation, and the manner in which she refused to let the tropic heat wilt her won his admiration.

He was suspecting that it was more than admiration he felt for her. As if his eyes had been opened, he said, "To give you courage, mavourneen? What words of mine could add to the fire in you? I said I love you, and what I said I meant!"

"And the Frenchwoman? Céleste d'Ogeron?"

The thought of pale Céleste sobered him. He drew back a little, and Lizzie, feeling him withdraw, shivered against the fright in her.

He said soberly, "I've promised to marry her, Lizzie."

She sighed and got to her feet. He could not see her face, but he saw the rigidity of the back she showed him. He put out a hand, but she moved away toward the little pallet of branches and leaves that formed her bed.

All the next day Martin Chandos moved close behind Lizzie, seeking for a moment when he might explain his words. He had lain on his back, staring up at the starry sky a long time after she was asleep. He had searched his soul to find the answer to the promise he had made Céleste d'Ogeron, and this wild contradiction of the flesh that urged him to sweep Lizzie Hollister into his arms. But Lizzie would have none of him. She kept to herself, and turned away her face when he would have spoken.

Toward evening, as they moved through a riotous tangle of orchid stems and fragrant hibiscus, Lizzie stumbled over a low *bejuco* vine. From his position behind her, Martin Chandos saw a flash of dull grayish green in the undergrowth at her side, and in that instant his pistol was in his hand.

He put a ball an inch from Lizzie's black hair, into the gaping mouth of a deadly green parrot snake.

He caught Lizzie up with his big hands and held her against him as she fought, hammering his thick chest with tiny fists. She had not seen the snake, nor did Martin Chandos think to show it to her at the moment. There was wild laughter in his throat as he tightened his arms and bent her, tight and helpless, to him.

He kissed her then, hotly and savagely, with something of the jungle's heat in him. She tried to struggle, but her muscles were no match for the arms banding her.

"Aye!" he panted as he kissed her. "I said I loved you, and by the silver hand of Nuada, it's the truth I spoke! You jungle witch! You white Venus! You hear me?"

She did not cease to struggle until his muscles and his kisses drained the strength from her. She clung to him, and slowly, as his lips moved from her throat to a little ear, she smiled.

"Céleste? What of Céleste, Martin?" she breathed.

"Hobgob fly off with her! It's yourself is my woman, Lizzie Hollister! I'm a fool not to have known it sooner!"

She turned then, wildly unashamed, and sought his lips with her own. They kissed until Redscar Hudson stooped under a poinsettia branch to grumble at them.

That night, and for two more nights, they slept side by side in the jungle heat, as chaste as children. Martin Chandos would not touch her, other than to drink kisses at the fountain of her mouth. "It's a cruel thing I do to myself and to you, acushla, but I'll wait until we're wed right and proper. Fash, it's a saint you're making of me, with this new kind of love!"

When he spoke like that her soft palm would stroke his cheek, her violet eyes grown dreamy, and the weight of her black head would droop to his shoulder as she fell asleep with his protecting arm about her.

They came into Puerto Bello on the heels of a mule train from Panama bringing silver wedges from Peru and golden ingots and emeralds from New Grenada. Little silver bells tinkled all along the Gold Road, which ran from Panama to Puerto Bello and its mile-long harbor, for this was late spring, the time for the great fair that brought traders from Panama and San Juan de Ulna and Santo Domingo. The silver and gold would be stacked high in the great marketplace to be shipped to the vessels of the fleet that swung at anchor before the forts.

Their three Itza guides had left them a few miles below the Gold Road, in a mangrove swamp from which Martin Chandos could see the towering bulks of the Puerto Bello forts of San Felipe de Sotomayor and Santiago de la Gloria.

No one heeded them as they followed the laden mules into the city proper at dusk, clad in borrowed finery looted from a small trading train. Their swift attack had gone unnoticed, for none suspected the presence of buccaneers this close to a Caribbean city. They passed the castle of San Jerónimo and moved on through the paved streets toward the rich mansions. They avoided the more crowded streets, seeking the shelter of the narrow alleys. They went swiftly, and since this was the time of the great fair and many inhabitants were abroad in the streets, they drew no attention.

They came at last to the warehouses fronting the harbor, great buildings of stone and wood, lacking ornamentation. A dagger picked a lock, and one by one they slipped in through the huge wooden doors. While the others crouched in the darkness, Martin Chandos drew Lizzie with him by a hand to the opposite end of the warehouse. The harbor lay like a pool of silver in the moonlight before their eyes.

He put his gaze to the ships at anchor, searching them one after the other. One galleon, tall and black, with sails furled on her yards and her giltwork glowing in the moonbeams, drew his regard. There was something about that ship that held his attention, something familiar but forgotten.

And then remembrance came to Martin Chandos and he stiffened, and soft laughter rose from his lips. "A jest of fate, Lizzie! That's the Vengador yonder. Don Carlos Esquivel Alcantara's ship. What irony that it should be his vessel that will be after carrying us all safely home to Tortugal!"

He began to strip off his satin-embroidered jerkin and
laced shirt, until he stood naked to the waist in breeches
and silk stockings. There was movement beside him and
he paused like that, to stare at Lizzie Hollister, who was
pulling her Spanish gown from her until she stood in her
Itza tunic, smiling up at him.

"I swim with you, Martin! Once I told you, your destiny is my destiny. That's the way it will always be."

"Ah, Lizzie! Your loveliness tears the heart from a
man!"

He put his arms around her and his mouth sought
hers, and it was with a catch of breath that he put her
from him. "I'll be in no mood to swim if we keep this
up, Lizzie darling! I don't suppose I can be after per-
suading you to stay behind, so come along!"

They hit the water in twin dives and swam side by side
across the harbor, from the stone wharf that flanked the
warehouse to the huge black bulk of the Vengador. They
heard no tramp of feet as they caught the anchor chain
and clung to it, listening.

"They're at the fair, enjoying themselves, so they are."
He laughed softly. "It's a pleasure I'm glad to grant them.
It gives us a free hand on the decks above. We'll not have
to go back for the others. We can take it ourselves."

He went first up the iron links and hung to the forerail
with an arm, sweeping the empty decks with his gaze.
Then he was bending and catching Lizzie by a wrist and
hauling her up to drip water on the boards beside him.
They moved together down the main deck to the hatches.
A quick inspection showed them the hold fitted for sea,
with water casks and tins of food stored beside barrels of
gunpowder and piled iron cannon balls.

"Don Carlos is a careful captain," he admitted. "It's
sorry I am that I can't stop to tell him how careful. But
I've others than myself to think about. A few moments
while we go aft to check the cabins. Then we'll have the
lads in the warehouse here to up anchor."

They were moving across the planks of the quarter-
deck when they heard low, sensual laughter. It froze
them like wet statues on either side of the whipstaff
hutch.

"A woman's laughter," whispered Lizzie.

"Aye, the way a woman laughs when a man begins to
please her. It comes from the Captain's cabin, Lizzie!

Now, it couldn't be that Don Carlos is in his cabin, could it?"

He went forward on wet, stockinged feet and the door pull of the cabin door was in his fingers and it was turning; and he stood there, staring into the stern cabin that was so brightly lighted with scores of tall candles.

Don Carlos Esquivel Alcantara was seated in a brocaded coronation chair, bending to caress a woman who gurgled laughter as her russet hair hung down from the crook of his arm.

It was as Don Carlos felt the wind through the doorway and lifted his lean face to stare at him that Martin Chandos remembered that he carried no weapon.

The woman slipped from the Spaniard's arms to the floor as Don Carlos came to his feet, reaching out for the rapier he had laid across his mahogany desk. Her laughter stilled to breathlessness as she caught her disarranged bodice about her shoulders. For an instant Martin Chandos saw her face, and something like shock ran through him.

"Ysabella de Sorolla!" he whispered.

Her hazel eyes went wide. The hand with which she held torn satin and laces to her bosom began to tremble. "*Por Dios!* You!"

Don Carlos scowled from the man in the doorway to the woman at his knees. "You know him, Ysabella?"

Doña Ysabella began to laugh, her head thrown back, her mouth open. "Know him? *Sí, sí!* I know him and so do you, Carlos! So does all Spain! He is Martin Chandos—Martín el Afortunado! The man whose back you whipped on the deck of the Forthright! It is a great jest, is it not?"

Don Carlos swore, his dark eyes blazing. His rapier lifted until it pointed at the Irishman. "*Hola!* I recognize him now!" Don Carlos also recognized the fact that Martin Chandos had no rapier, no cutlass, no boarding pistol at hand.

The big Irishman was cursing the impetuosity that had sent him into the water without a weapon. He had not meant to come up on the deck of the Vengador, but only to spy out her guards. But her silence and seeming desertion had allured him, and now he stood with his big chest naked to the point that Don Carlos was bringing ever closer to his skin.

Don Carlos laughed and lunged, but Martin Chandos was dropping, clawing out at the other's booted foot with a hooking hand. His fingertips slid across red leather, and then he was rolling on, to bring up against a big rosewood sea chest. His hunting hand found a silver candelabra, and he hurled it at the Spaniard.

Don Carlos chuckled. His black eyes burned. "Lock the door, Ysabella," he whispered.

Martin Chandos heard the key grate, and from the corners of his eyes he saw Doña Ysabella standing with her back to the door, dropping the key out of sight in her bodice. But that act was the tinder that lit a fire in Lizzie Hollister.

She came out of the shadows and her Itza tunic flapped wildly as she catapulted into the Spanish woman. Her lithe brown fingers went into the mass of hair and she tugged, and as Doña Ysabella screamed, Lizzie opened her mouth and her white teeth lunged, biting.

In a moment the two women were rolling over and over across the cabin carpet, nails ripping, teeth bared, their clothes shredding under clawing fingers. Awed by their fury, Don Carlos and Martin Chandos watched for a moment.

It was the Spaniard who turned from them first. His long fingers tightened on the haft of his sword and he slid forward, the blade held out before him. He whispered through thinned lips, "And now to butcher you for the Irish pig you are!"

Martin Chandos snatched up a footstool and used it to fend off the blade, but it was lightning in the candlelight, darting here, then there. He felt it like white-hot iron as it drew blood from his forearm.

He leaped for the great desk, vaulting it, placing it between him and the Spaniard. His eyes roved the cabin desperately.

And then he saw it, hanging on the wall.

A length of pliant black bullhide, plaited and woven, with a horn handle. It was not the whip that had scourged him over the cannon on the Forthright, but it was a weapon. He reached it in two bounds and jerked it down.

Don Carlos saw his move with wide eyes, and cursed the cruelty in him that had insisted he toy with this Irish demon before killing him. To make amends for that hesitation, he came running, intent only on plunging his blade into the other's middle.

It had been a long time since Martin Chandos had felt a whip handle in his fingers. In his youth, on his father's Galway farm, he had practiced its art with old Conal to guide him, but he was rusty in its use.

He made up for that clumsiness by sheer strength. He sent the black lash whirling out so that it caught and tangled across Don Carlos' middle. With a wrench, before the whip could uncoil, he yanked him sideways, and went to meet him with a balled fist. He swung with all the power of his big frame.

Had his fist landed, he would have broken the Spaniard's jaw. But Don Carlos moved too swiftly, darting aside and thrusting.

His blade dug across Martin Chandos' ribs, leaving a stream of blood trickling down his flesh. His laughter grew feverish. He came like a bull, head lowered, sword out ahead of him. Martin Chandos side-stepped and went back to gain room. His arm rose and the black lash snaked overhead and then went out in a straight line at the Spaniard. It coiled around his face, biting. And then it was flying high again and coming down, and now it tore his velvet doublet in half and clung with hot fire to his ribs.

Don Carlos stumbled. The lash was a flying flame that tore at thighs and chest. Once it whipped around his face, slicing flesh. He screamed, lunging with his sword at this dancing giant whose right hand lifted and fell as it sent that black coil of bullhide flying and dancing.

There was no escape from that whip. It found him at chest and leg, face and neck, and roused an insane fire in him. He hurtled forward at Martin Chandos where the Irishman stood before the sloping windows of the stern cabin, and this time the whip did not stop him.

His blade before him, Don Carlos crashed into the windows. They broke, tinkling, but the leaded frames held him a moment, poised there above the gallery and the sternposts.

And then he was falling through the night, and his scream was lost in a rush of wind. His body hit the gallery rail with a thud and a break of bones. And then he toppled over, bounced on the curving rudder, and slid into the black, oily waters of the harbor.

Martin Chandos hung in the smashed window, staring down at the trail of bubbles that broke, one after the other, until only the smooth swell of water remained.

With a sigh he turned back into the room, where Lizzie Hollister was rising from an inert Doña Ysabella. Her Itza tunic was gone, and she poised there, watching his eyes go over her. Then she bent and swept up the brocaded cloak that Doña Ysabella had worn to the Vengador earlier that evening, and wrapped it around her.

Her eyes glowed at him over the furred collar. "You bring the men, Martin. I'll have to find something in which to clothe myself. Then I'll join you."

They carried the unconscious Doña Ysabella to the tender that bumped its prow against the curving hull of the black galleon. She did not waken until Martin Chandos lifted her out onto the cobblestones of the warehouse wharf and set her on her feet. Lizzie, clad in borrowed shirt and breeches, handed her the cloak.

Lizzie Hollister and Martin Chandos stood and watched Doña Ysabella de Sorolla walk forever out of their lives. Then, hand in hand, they went into the dark warehouse.

Excited whispers met their ears. Hands came out of the darkness into the moonlight that flooded the open warehouse door, hands that were thick with necklaces of giant rosy pearls, laden with diamonds, hands that cupped yellow doubloons and pieces of eight.

"Treasure, Martin!" whispered Redscar Hudson hoarsely. "The treasure the Spaniards took off their fleet ships, so they could come out and trap us off Raven Island! They substituted lead ingots for this stuff, you'll mind."

He remembered the sight of the three Spanish galleons dumping those lead ingots, which he had thought were gold at first, into the waters of the Caribbean. He laughed softly at the trick an ironic fate had played.

"Over here," said another voice in the blackness. "Trunks on trunks of the yellow boys, just beggin' to be took!"

They showed him, dancing before him in their eagerness, opening trunk lids to paw at coins and jewels, thrusting coffers of brilliant diamonds to his gaze. He saw gold and silver, pearls and diamonds and emeralds. The size of the fortune dizzied him, for this was the yield for an entire year, from the Pearl Coast of the Orinoco westward into the Inca cities of Peru, and northward through the gold-mine country to Vera Cruz.

"Lay hands on it," he told them. "Carry it as you can. Every man take hold of something. We'll teach the Spaniards to play tricks on Martín el Afortunado!"

Laughter rose hot and thick in the dark warehouse. Feet slapped on the floor boards as they ran eagerly to do his bidding. Redscar Hudson took a dozen men at his heels and went up and down the quay, taking idle boats. Inside an hour théy were leaving the black warehouse behind them, their pinnaces and tenders almost awash with the weight of the treasure they carried.

It lacked an hour of dawn when the capstan bars of the Vengador began to rattle as her anchor rose deckward. From the rail, where he leaned with Lizzie, Martin Chandos could see the sweep of deck below, where the freedmen from the mines ran to Redscar's bellow, the mixture of Englishmen and Frenchmen, Dutchmen and Scots. It was as if he could see their sons and their sons' sons in his mind, for in this great new world those men below would marry Irish girls and German, French girls and English, Dutch and Italian. Their descendants would be members of a strong, new breed of men on the earth.

"Americans," whispered Martin Chandos, and drew Lizzie against him. "They'll father a new race, those men. Not just one nationality, but a mixture of all of them. Just as we'll be doing ourselves, Lizzie darling."

The Vengador slid silently past Fort Santiago de la Gloria in the last pall of darkness, as the first ribbons of red dawn fire were lighting the horizon eastward, painting the man and woman at the quarter rail in scarlet. Lizzie stirred. "What of Céleste, Martin? What will we tell her?"

Martin Chandos scowled. "The truth, Lizzie. But I don't like to think about how she'll take it. I'd rather face Don Carlos' sword than her accusing eyes."

Chapter Fifteen

CÉLESTE D'OGERON widened her eyes as Martin Chandos came into the library of the Governor's mansion with Lizzie Hollister on his arm. She took one incredulous look at the manner in which they held hands, then stared frankly at the girl.

Lizzie Hollister wore a gown of white satin faced with frilled blue bows and forget-me-nots. Blue gloves fitted her forearms, to disappear under the ruffled sleeves. She was no pirate wench now, but a great lady, with her chin held high and proud as her violet eyes challenged the astonished Frenchwoman.

Céleste d'Ogeron turned her gaze from Lizzie to stare upward at her father. He stood by her chair, his hand tight on its high back, his face darkened by a scowl.

Beyond her father the Vicomte de Piercy stood with a hand lifted to his cravat, his dark eyes shining as they began to understand the emotion filling these two people. As he watched, his hard mouth curved into a smile.

Bertrand d'Ogeron had not missed the significance of those entwined fingers either. "Well, Martin?" he said. "I've heard of your venture. How you freed the men in the mines. How you killed Don Carlos in a duel. How you fell face first, practically, into as vast a treasure as you ever brought to Tortuga. And now—"

Martin Chandos was aware that his heart hammered in his chest. His tongue was thick in his mouth, and he could feel Lizzie's fingers trembling in his own.

"M'sieu d'Ogeron, you've been correctly informed. But I came myself to tell you the most important news of all."

Céleste d'Ogeron stilled the movement of her fan. Over its laced rim she stared at Lizzie Hollister, with wonder in her eyes.

Martin Chandos drew a deep breath. He said loudly, against the nervousness in him, "I have the honor to wed Elizabeth Hollister this evening at my home. I invite you and Mademoiselle Céleste to the ceremony."

Bertrand d'Ogeron exclaimed, "Wed Lizzie! But you're engaged to Céleste! *Corbleu!* I consider this— I can't believe—"

He went no further. Céleste came out of her chair to stand with her eyes big and wide. She whispered softly, "Martin! You've made me so happy!"

Martin Chandos gaped at her, aware that his lower jaw was open. "Happy?" he repeated in surprise.

The Vicomte came forward, brushing past the Governor, a hand outheld to the Irishman. "Accept my felicitations, m'sieu. It takes courage to do what you have done. More courage, perhaps, than to take your ship into battle. Courage I should like to see in myself."

The Governor broke in on these congratulations, growling savagely. "It is an insult you do my family, Martin Chandos! To have my daughter scorned—"

Martin Chandos shook himself. The nervousness that had been in him as he steeled himself to face Céleste d'Ogeron was gone, washed away in her obvious delight. He was not nervous as he turned to her father. His reaction was turning to anger.

"Fash, now! Can you so consider it, with your daughter in tears of joy? If she tells me I've insulted her, I'll do something to make amends."

Céleste dabbed at her eyes with a silk kerchief. "Insult me? You've set me free! Free to marry whom I will! Free to ignore the protests of my father, who sees in me only a chattel to be sold to the richest man in sight!"

She drew a deep breath and swung about to face the darkly scowling Governor. Her head went back as her blue eyes blazed. "Yes, I've been a prisoner! Tell them, dear Papa, how you kept me in my room while Martin Chandos was in Tortuga after sinking the Victoire and the Hussy! How you delivered the flowers he sent me every day with a lecture on the rights of fathers, and the obedience with which a dutiful daughter must wed the man her father chooses!

"I saw no one. I might as well have been in the Bastille! 'Marry this Martin Chandos, and be rich! Take him to France! Or else he and his ships will drive Spain out of the Caribbean and destroy the sweet trade that makes me rich!' Always he thinks of his purse, does Papa."

The Vicomte stepped to her side, placing an arm about her waist. His dark eyes glowed with the courage he was taking from the example of this buccaneer captain. "Tell them, m'sieu," he said quietly. "Tell them how you forbade me your house, forbade me to see the woman I love. You sought to break her will, the will of my Céleste! You nearly did, for she agreed to wed with Martin."

Céleste lifted her eyes to the tall nobleman at her side. Her hand pressed his, to lend reassurance. She said, "Yes, I was ready to marry him, after Raoul Sans Espoir and Lizzie returned from their fateful voyage—when Martin kissed my ear.

"It was the deciding straw. I thought of my dear Pierre, whom I loved, and I lost my head. I raged at you, dear Martin, sent you back to sea. Again my father imprisoned me, until I did break. When you returned and sought my hand in marriage, I agreed. But how many times did I cry myself to sleep at night on my pillow!"

Martin Chandos glowered at Bertrand d'Ogeron. "I was a blind fool. Not only about Lizzie, but about this other matter. Lizzie would not have been so patient to find that I was putting off to sea without marrying her. She'd have married me and come along."

Céleste swung about. "Martin, I could not help being delighted when you postponed our marriage yourself. Now, Papa, you can have no objection to my taking the first ship back to France, and marrying my Pierre."

The Governor shrugged his shoulders. "What can one say? If Martin marries Lizzie, all the world will know that Céleste has been jilted, and how then will I find a rich husband for her? All right, all right, marry your Pierre!"

The Vicomte gasped and his arm squeezed tighter around Céleste's yielding waist. "Darling, did you hear?"

Céleste blinked back sudden tears, tears that were a reaction to her sudden French emotionalism. She stepped into her father's arms, which caught and hugged her. He patted her shoulder, smiling wryly.

"It is time I returned to France, anyhow," he said. "I will become a senile old man, and sit in the sun and play with my grandchildren." He held out a hand to the Vicomte, who clasped it strongly.

Martin Chandos grinned. "No need for that. Lizzie and I won't stay here. We sail north to New Amsterdam with Redscar Hudson and my old Forthright crew. They want to settle there and become farmers or merchants, and I'll do the same. The English have taken over the place, and I hear they're thinking of calling it New York. It's a new name for an old town, a good omen for a man and woman about to begin a new life themselves!"

Sails flapped overhead, and under his booted feet he could feel the forward surge of the black Vengador as it slid through the cresting waves of the Atlantic. Ahead lay New Amsterdam and a new life. Behind him was his career as buccaneer.

Behind him too, was his marriage to Lizzie Hollister in the house on the Tortuga hillside, and the party that had followed it. He had crept away from that party with Lizzie in her bridal gown, to find sanctuary on the deserted Vengador.

A smile touched his lips when he thought of that night. His wife had been a witch-woman in the moonlight that flooded the deserted decks, running ahead of him, kicking off her slippers as she ran.

Her laughter had been warm and rousing. In the cabin door he had paused amazed, for Lizzie had pulled off her dress and stood facing him in the tattered shirt and tight black breeks she had worn under it, barefoot, her shimmering black hair undone and cascading over her shoulders.

"For the last time I am your pirate wench, Martin! With this new wifehood, I am putting all that behind me. But for tonight I am Lizzie!"

His lips curved in a faint remembering smile. Ah, she had been the teasing hoyden, the laughing temptress! In the silvery moonlight filtering through the stern cabin windows she had clung to him and wept with happiness, and Martin Chandos had felt the stirrings of a man newly born to life.

As he lounged here at the taffrail, he heard a footfall and turned. Lizzie was walking toward him—no, not Lizzie, but Elizabeth, Mistress Chandos, in a crisply starched gray dress with a Holland linen band at her waist. She wore a linen cap over her black hair, and sensible walking shoes appeared under the hem of her long skirt.

The wind stirred her gown as she came to stand beside him. He put an arm around her soft waist and drew her close against him. Together they stared out over the waves toward the new life that lay before them.

"New Amsterdam," she whispered, eyes shining. "It's yonder, Martin, waiting for us!"

THE END
of a novel by
Gardner F. Fox